THE STICK HANDLER

CATHRYN FOX

COPYRIGHT

The Stick Handler
Copyright 2018 by Cathryn Fox
Published by Cathryn Fox

This e-book is licensed for your personal enjoyment only. This e-book may not be re-sold or given away to other people. If you would like to share this book with another person, please purchase an additional copy for each recipient. If you're reading this book and did not purchase it, or it was not purchased for your use only, then please return to your favorite e-book retailer and purchase your own copy. Thank you for respecting the hard work of this author.

ISBN Print: 978-1-928056-95-9
ISBN ebook: 978-1-928056-96-6

"It's over, Arianna."

"Over?" she spits out, her eyes venomous as they hold my stare. "Oh, we're far from over, Luke." As I square off against Arianna in her waterfront suite, the moonlight shimmering on Seattle's Elliot Bay below, she points a finger at me, then wags it back and forth between the two of us. "In fact, you and me, we're just beginning." With that, she gives a defiant lift of her chin and flicks her long blonde hair over her shoulder, a dismissive gesture that I've grown accustomed to over the last six months. "Now go home, get a good night's sleep and I'll see you at the altar tomorrow afternoon." She offers me her back and picks up her champagne glass, shutting me out, and this conversation down.

I glance at my watch, take in the late hour. Yeah, okay, putting the brakes on our relationship the night before our wedding is a dick move on my part, but isn't it better to make a clean break now, before we find ourselves old and miserable and totally hating each other? Come to think of it, do we even like each other now?

"Ari—"

She spins to face me. "Do you need a Midol, or something?"

For fuck's sake. "No, I don't need a goddamn Midol."

"Then stop acting like you're PMS'ing!" she shouts back.

I shake my head. She might be a girl used to getting what she wants, but after overhearing her tell her friend she doesn't love me, and revealing a few other facts that surprised the shit out of me, she can't expect me to show up for the ceremony tomorrow. You'd think I'd be furious to find out her true feelings, right? But the funny thing is, I'm not really angry or upset at all, which says lot about the state of our relationship. I guess I'm grateful that I walked into the room during her private conversation. It snapped me the fuck out of the damn trance I'd been in for the last few months.

"You and I both know this is a mistake," I say.

"A mistake?" she seethes. "How can you say that?" She finishes the champagne in her glass and struts to her kitchen to refill it. I pace her living room, glance out the floor-to-ceiling window. My gaze goes to the spectacular view of the waterfront ferris wheel at Pier 57, with the Washington state ferry in the background. Too bad I can't quite seem to enjoy the Seattle Great Wheel, beautifully lit up this time of night. The tapping of Ari's shoes reaches my ears as she comes back into the room.

"Why are you still here?" she asks.

"Because this conversation isn't over." I spin and point to the cellphone that never leaves her hand. "You just told your best friend that love isn't important in a marriage."

She glares at me for a long moment, the anger leaving her baby blues as dark lashes fall slowly, only to flicker back open over come-hither eyes. "Luke, honey, you know I love you. What I said, it's just that Kari is just jealous of our relationship and I was being flippant. You know, to ease her pain, because she'll never have what we have, baby."

"What exactly do we have?" It's a question I'd been asking myself all day, long before I ever learned Ari valued money over love.

She sets her glass down and sidles up to me, rubbing her lithe body against mine, another little ploy she uses when things aren't going her way. "Together we can have it all. Remember that first weekend we spent in Boston?"

Boston? Oh yeah, I remember Boston. Remember opening the door to my hotel room after our game, and finding a naked Ari on my bed. I thought I was concussing. That maybe I'd taken one too many hits to the head earlier that night. Either that, or she'd stumbled into the wrong room. I was a rookie, and a girl like Ari, well, she could have any guy on the team—one with much more power and play than me. But no, she assured me it was the Stick Handler she was looking for—my on-ice nickname.

I wasn't sure why she'd set her sights on me, and before I knew it, a few months had passed and she was planning an elaborate spring wedding, as soon as hockey season ended. I'm not even sure I ever asked her to marry me. But the next thing I knew we were picking out a ring, and tasting pound cake with buttery icing.

I scrub the back of my neck, work out the knots. "Ari—"

Her hands go to my face, and she presses her lips to mine. "Our wedding is tomorrow Luke. Now is not the time to be getting cold feet."

"It's not cold feet. I just heard you tell your friend I would make a suitable husband because I could keep you in the lifestyle you're accustomed to." Hell, maybe she picked me because, as the daughter of the man who owns the Seattle Shooters, she had insider information, knew I was about to land a significant contract and become one of the highest paid guys in the NHL. She sure as hell didn't pick me out of love.

I shake my head, hating that I let things get so out of hand, that I let her lead me like a lamb to the slaughter. I'm a grown fucking man who can make his own decisions, so why the hell did I just go along with her, cave to everything she wanted? Oh, maybe because it was easier to be with Ari, and go with the flow—keep my mind off the one girl I've always loved, the girl who'd grown up next door to me, and who keeps me in the friend zone.

But now, I just can't bring myself to go through with this marriage. We both know we're not in love, and we'd be making a big mistake if we exchanged vows tomorrow. I remove her arms from my neck and place them at her sides. Her fingers grip her phone tighter, and her mood darkens.

I exhale slowly. "Why don't you call your friends. Have them come stay the night." I might not love her, but I care about her. And even though she just admitted she didn't love me, that months ago her father threatened to cut up her credit cards if she didn't settle herself into a career, I'm still a decent human being who doesn't want to see anyone upset.

"You can't do this to me," she says, her voice bordering on hysterical.

"Please, Ari." I put my hand on her arm, give it a reassuring squeeze. "You know in your heart this isn't right. You'll find the perfect guy for you in time." Although with her father threatening to cut up her credit cards, time is not on her side. I guess that's why she latched on to me so quick. She was desperate for a rich daddy figure who would help her keep the socialite lifestyle she's grown accustomed to, and never make her work for anything she wants. It's a role I can no longer go along with.

She steps away, and her high heels wobble slightly as she paces to her window. With her back to me, she says, "You're making a big mistake."

There is a calculated coldness in her tone that raises the hair on my arms. "I'm sorry, Ari. I never meant to hurt you."

"Hurt me?" she shrieks. "You're the one who's going to be hurt, Luke." She spins, and her eyes narrow in on me. Jesus, if looks could kill. "If you do this, I'll make sure you never play hockey for the Shooters again."

My heart jumps into my throat. Does she have the power to do that? Yeah, she's the owner's daughter, but can she pull his strings, too? Fuck, maybe she can. She sure as hell pulled mine for the last few months.

"If you don't want me to destroy you and your reputation, I suggest you accept what I'm about to offer." She folds her arms, and the pale blue dress she's wearing climbs up her thighs. Since I'm a guy who loves a nice pair of legs, maybe she's doing it on purpose, to lure me with sex like she did that first night in Boston. I fell for it once, and look where that led me. Then again, is the fault entirely hers? I went along with it, which means half the responsibility is mine. "Are you listening to me, Luke?"

I brace myself, almost afraid to hear her offer. "I'm listening."

"Good. Take a week. Go, get your head on right."

"Jesus, Ari, my head is on right."

"No, it's not, otherwise you wouldn't be putting your career on the line like this. I can destroy you, Luke." She snaps her fingers for effect. "Like this!"

Who the hell is *this* woman? For the last six months, she'd been nothing but charming. Then again, I'd given her everything she wanted, until now. Even before I heard her say those things to her friend, I knew I couldn't go through with it, not when my heart belongs to another—despite the fact that I can never have her. Christ, what kind of fucked up mess have I gotten myself in to?

"Why would you want to do destroy me, Ari?"

She stands a little straighter. "Because no one embarrasses Arianna Moore. No one."

"Fine, we'll tell everyone it was your idea. That you broke things off."

"What we'll do is tell everyone I needed time to think. In the meantime, you have one week. One week to think about this mistake you're making, the future that will be ripped right out from underneath you if you don't do the right thing."

I'm not a violent man. Jonah, aka the Body Checker, takes care of anyone who gets in the way of my stick-handling skills, but suddenly my fingers are curling, the urge to put my fist though her wall pulling at me hard. I grew up with nothing, and spent my whole life working my fucking ass off, practicing every goddamn night, until I was good enough to be scouted at the Junior A level. My scholarship to Arizona State gave me a top-notch education and I made a name for myself in the rink. No fucking way am I about to let her destroy my reputation and take that all away from me, simply because she wants to save face. We're not right for each other and we both know it.

"One week," she says again. "Use our honeymoon tickets and get away for a bit, to think this over, and you tell no one what's really going on. No one. Not even that tomboy you hang around with, otherwise...." Her words fall off as she snaps her fingers again.

"Her name is Katee, and she's not a tomboy."

She rolls her eyes at me. "Whatever. Do we have a deal?"

I'm about to argue, but stop to think about that for a moment. Maybe a week away will do her good. Giver her clarity and help her see the mistake we'd be making if we went through with this.

"Fine," I say. "One week. Then we'll talk."

A small, triumphant smile tweaks the corners of her lips.

She obviously thinks she won the battle. I can only hope that after seven days, she comes to the same conclusion that I have. Still grinning at me, she slides her fingers across her phone, and puts it to her ear.

"Kari, I've been thinking." A big sigh, followed by a long pause for effect, then she continues with, "I'm not so sure about tomorrow." I stand there, taking in her expert performance as she tells Kari she might need more time before she walks down the aisle with me. Her best friend Kari is a blogger and a socialite. In all of five minutes, I expect the entire world to know that my fiancée has decided to postpone the wedding.

I leave her luxurious penthouse apartment, a headache brewing as I dig my phone out to call my folks and the guys who were standing up for me. I make the calls as I wait for the elevator, and oddly enough, no one seems surprised. My folks almost seem happy about it. I'm not sure they were ever big fans of Ari's anyway. The elevator arrives, and I step on and make my way to the garage. I have one last call to make, the most important call, but I'll do that from the privacy of my car. As soon as I step off, my phone pings. Dammit. I am not in the mood to answer any more questions tonight. I pull the phone from my pocket, about to power it down when I see who the text is from. My heart pounds a little faster, and no matter how much of a shit mood I'm in, Katee's texts always brighten my day.

I just heard the news, where are you?

KATEE

I hold my phone in my hand, my heart racing as I wait for Luke to reply. What the hell was Ari thinking, postponing the wedding at the eleventh hour because she was having second thoughts for reasons she doesn't want disclosed to the public. I wasn't too crazy about my best friend's fiancée before tonight and now, I hate her just a little bit more.

I rush around my apartment looking for my damn car keys. I don't care if it's late, Luke needs me, and no matter what, I'll always be there for him. Ever since he punched that bully on the playground and stood up for me, we've been the best of friends. I can't even imagine how devastated he must be. The news is all over Kari's blog, and because Ari is being so secretive, I'm sure half of Seattle suspects Luke was unfaithful. Every single player on the team has a reputation with the ladies. But I know Luke. I know he's a one-woman kind of guy and isn't a player off the ice, like the rest of his teammates. This must be so mortifying for him. As my heart aches for my best friend, my phone finally pings.

I'm on my way home. You don't need to come over.

I read his text, and my fingers fly over my phone. *Like hell. I'm on my way now.*

I find my keys at the bottom of my gym bag, and rush out the door. Since I have no time—or the patience—to wait for the slow-ass elevator to arrive, I take the stairs three at a time, and nearly tumble down the last flight when my foot goes out from beneath me. Damn slippery floors! Rain falls heavily as I push through the lobby door, soaking me to my skin as I race for my car. I climb inside and turn on the heat. Dammit, in my hurry, I forgot to grab my coat. I've only been in Seattle for a year, moving here to be closer to my best friend after he signed a contract with the Shooters, and I'm still not used to the weather. I jack the heat higher and back out into the street. Ten minutes later, I pull in to Luke's spare parking spot outside his apartment building.

I jump from the car and hurry inside the building. I press his button and he buzzes me up. I take his elevator to the penthouse suite and his door is open, welcoming me. For some reason, that always brings a smile to my face. It falls quickly when I remember why I'm here.

"Luke," I say and enter his place to find him standing by his window, a beer bottle dangling from his fingers.

"Hey," he says and taps his bottle against his leg. Worried eyes rake over me, take in my drenched, see-through blouse. "You're soaked."

"Way to state the obvious." I pull my wet shirt from my skin and as it makes a sucking noise, I shiver from the cold. "What the hell happened?"

"You read Kari's blog, I take it."

I nod. "Why does she need time to think about things? You're the best thing that has ever happened to that girl. Why is she getting cold feet now?"

He opens his mouth like he wants to tell me something, but shuts it again. What the hell? What is it he doesn't want to say? We've always been honest with each other. "What?" I ask.

He produces two e-tickets from his back pocket. "Want to go on my honeymoon with me?" He laughs, but it holds no humor. The poor guy is really hurting. I glance at the tickets as he tosses them onto his coffee table.

He's joking about me going, I know, but maybe getting away from here, from the rumors that are sure to spread, will do him good. As the cold rain seeps under my skin and chills me to the bones, I bend to read the e-tickets.

"You need to get out of those clothes." His voice sounds tortured and once again my heart goes out to him.

"You're right." I pop the buttons on my blouse. "I was in such a hurry, I forgot my coat, and my umbrella broke in the last wind storm." Then again, I'm used to being wet since I moved to Seattle from Texas. I peel my blouse from my shoulders, and reach for the button on my jeans.

"You didn't have to rush over here. I'm fine."

"You just got dumped the night before your wedding. Of course, I had to rush over here. You need me." I wiggle my hips, but the damn wet jeans won't budge. "They're stuck to me." I shoot him a pleading glance. "Can you help?" He scrubs his chin and I wiggle some more.

"Here," he says and goes to his knees before me. I grip his shoulder to hang on as he tugs. I move my hips and try to help. "Stay still," he grumbles. "This is hard enough as it is."

He's not normally grumpy with me, but I can understand his irritability. He must be devastated by the turn of events. He finally gets my pants to my ankles, and I lift one foot then the other.

"Much better," I say, as he gathers my clothes and takes them to the dryer.

"I'll get you a towel." He disappears down the hall and comes back with a big fluffy towel. "Here."

He tosses it to me, and doesn't bother to avert his gaze as I dry my body. I rub my hair before bending forward, sticking my ass in the air as I twirl the cotton around the wet strands. My eyes go back to his, take in the way he's looking at my near nudity. Seeing each other naked is nothing new. When I first moved to Seattle, I shared this place with Luke and he walked in on me a time or two when I was changing. When he had emergency appendectomy at Arizona State, I flew out to take care of him. I even helped him wash, and changed his clothes. It was impossible not to see him naked. But none of that matters because we don't look at each other with interest, or inappropriate thoughts. No, we're friends, best friends, and we don't think about each other as anything other than that.

Not that he would look at me like I was a woman, anyway. I'm sure he still sees me as that chubby girl from the playground. I might have lost the weight, but I'll never be as lithe or paper-thin as Arianna, or any of the other girls he's been with over the years. I'm far from his type, but that's okay, though. I'm happy with who I am, and it would be weird if Luke stopped treating me like one of the guys. I actually like being one of the guys, and always preferred climbing trees to playing with dolls.

"I'll get you a shirt," he says.

"Just give me yours." I love wearing his clothes, love the way they smell after they've been on his body.

He tugs it off, and I pull it on, breathing in his scent. I plant my hands on my hips and glance around his suite. Okay, what can I do to cheer up my best friend? "Want to get drunk, and have a Die Hard marathon?" I ask.

He laughs. "No."

I pick up the e-tickets, look them over again and check

out the destination. Cortina d'Ampezzo, Italy. "I get that you were kidding, but maybe we shouldn't let these tickets go to waste."

He angles his head, a smile playing with the corners of his mouth. Dammit, he doesn't need to fake a smile with me, doesn't need to hide the pain of his breakup.

"You want to go on my honeymoon with me, Katee?"

"To be honest, I'd rather go to Bali." I shake my head. "Who the hell would choose skiing on the slopes over a bikini on the beach?"

"Not me."

I toss the ticket back to the table, like they're diseased. "Then why did you agree to this?"

He opens his mouth, but closes it again and instead of answering, he pinches the bridge of his nose. "Maybe I could use another drink," he says. He seems to be hedging a lot tonight, but I'll give him that. The break-up might just be too fresh to talk about.

"I'll get it." I walk to his kitchen, and grab two beers. I twist off the lids and hand one to him. As he takes a big swallow and downs half the liquid, I look at him, really look at him. Jesus, his shoulders are so tight they're practically touching his ears, and if he clenches any harder he's going to crack his teeth.

"Sit," I say and point to his sofa. "Your muscles are so tight, you're about to snap."

He walks to the sofa and a little sigh catches in my throat. Yeah, I know. We don't look at each other with interest, but how can I not admire a work of art when I see it? I take a big sip from my bottle, set it down and place my hands on his shoulders. The second I touch him, he tenses even more.

"You're in bad shape, Luke."

"Yeah," he grumbles, his voice dropping an octave. "Tell me something I don't know."

I work my fingers into the knots, and they soften beneath me. As a massage therapist—specializing in sports therapy—and Luke's own personal masseuse, I intimately know every inch of his body. Well, not intimately in the way lovers know each other. I almost laugh at the thought of us being lovers. Ludicrous, right?

"That feels so good," he mumbles and lets his head fall back. His mouth parts, exposing perfect white teeth. I let my gaze move over his face as his lids droop over deep blue eyes. How could Arianna be having second thoughts? Not only is Luke the nicest looking guy I've ever seen he has a good heart and would move mountains for those he cares about. I, of all people, know that. I was a chubby girl with a learning disability when I was young, but he saw past that, saw me for who I really was, and he liked that girl. When I was diagnosed with dyslexia, he learned everything he could about my disability, and I swear to God, I only made it through high school because of him. He pushed me, studied with me, and never gave up on me. When I didn't have a date for the prom, he went with me, even though his friends teased him about it. But Luke never cared what other people said about him. If they said anything bad about me, however, they usually ended up with a black eye, and that was saying something, since Luke doesn't much care for violence. But when push comes to shove, he'll shove.

"This position isn't working." I run my fingers down his arms, and he moans his approval.

"Oh, it's working."

I laugh at that. "I can't reach your back. Let's move this into the bedroom."

"My bedroom?"

"Yeah, my massage table is in the car, and I'm not running back out there. I have no interest in getting wet again."

A strange groan sounds in his throat. "I'm okay. You don't need to give me a massage."

"Yes, I do. Now get up." I shove his shoulder, but he doesn't budge.

"Why are you so bossy?"

I laugh at that. "Would you want me any other way?"

"No, you're perfect just the way you are."

I whack him. "Yeah right," I say. He's always saying things like that to me. But we both know my flaws. "Get up."

He climbs from the sofa and my eyes go to his chest. My God, the man really does have a beautiful body. I sigh, and follow him into his room. He flicks the lamp beside the bed on, flops down onto the mattress and buries his face in his pillow. Since it's too difficult to work all angles from a standing position, I pull the towel off my head, and climb on top of him. Another little groan rumbles in the depths of his throat as my knees tighten around his sides.

"I know. I know. I'm not a lightweight. You don't have to drive the point home by groaning."

"I told you. You're perfect just the way you are. Why don't you believe me?" I wiggle until I'm settled on his firm backside.

His muscles ripple as I place my hands on him, working them over his body until he's a little looser beneath me. "Luke."

"Mmm..."

"I really am sorry about tonight," I say quietly. I don't want to press if he doesn't want to talk about this, but this is my best friend and I'm here to listen if he needs me. "Do you have any idea why Arianna needs time to think?"

He goes quiet. Too quiet, and once again I get the strange sense there is something he's not telling me.

"I think a week to think is going to do us both good," he finally says.

"I'm sure she'll come to her senses," I say. When Luke moved away to Arizona State, I was lost without him. Sure, I was busy getting my massage therapy certification, but my nights and weekends were lonely. I'd spent so much time at the rink watching him practice or play, I'd found myself wandering over, just to feel close to him. "After one week away, I'm positive Arianna will realize her mistake."

"I hope so," he says, and once again my heart breaks for him.

"Maybe you should go on your honeymoon. It's all booked, and I can't see the sense in letting it go to waste."

He turns his head, and I work on his other shoulder. "I don't even like skiing."

"I don't even know how, and will probably break my neck if I tried. But I'll go with you. If you want. We can take lessons, or find other things to keep ourselves occupied."

He shifts beneath me, and I go up on my knees as he rolls until I'm straddling him from above. "Oh yeah?"

"Lots of things. We always have fun together, no matter what we do. Besides, if Ari's stupid enough to postpone the wedding, then she doesn't deserve to go on any honeymoon with you—skiing or beach," I blurt out without thinking. Shit, I shouldn't have said that, but I'm angry, dammit. I might not like Arianna, but Luke is in love with her and that's all that matters.

I fall forward, and lay my head on his chest, revel in his strong heartbeat beneath my cheek. This is one of my favorite positions with Luke. Many times, over the years, we've laid like this, and his heartbeat always makes me feel so safe and secure. His hand goes to my hair and he strokes the damp strands down my back, his calluses scraping against my flesh. I shiver from his touch, and he grabs the blankets and pulls them over me. I close my eyes for a brief second and as sleep pulls at me, I stifle a yawn.

"We booked the honeymoon package," he whispers, his voice groggy. "Lots of events with other newlyweds."

"So."

"I'm not interested in explaining to anyone why I'm on my honeymoon with my best friend, not my new wife."

"No one has to know. Besides it's Italy, no one is going to recognize you there."

Luke's hand slides lower on my back and his breath is hot on my face when I lift my head to see him. "We could have some fun and pretend we're the newlyweds," I say, wanting to lighten his mood. God, I hate seeing him like this.

He rakes a hand through his hair, pushing it off his face. "You want to pretend to be my wife?" he asks, with a quirk of his brow. It's that sexy look right there that has women throwing their panties onto the ice.

"Sure, why not." I shrug. "It could be fun, actually."

"I thought you were anti-marriage," he says.

I frown. Luke knows all about my father leaving my mother for another woman. It devastated Mom and me, but fortunately Luke was there to help put me back together. He was there again after high school when he was home for Christmas and the guy I was dating at the local technical college fooled around with another one of our classmates. Are there no faithful guys out there? I only know of one, and he's off limits. Not that I think of him as more, anyway.

"You know I don't trust guys," I mumble.

"You trust me, don't you?"

I yawn, unable to hold it back any longer. "Of course. But you're not a real guy."

"Ah, I'm kind of a real guy, Katee." He lifts his hips, and I feel the Stick Handler's...stick. Wait, is he semi-hard? Curious, I move a bit, and he groans, shifting me until my weight is half on his leg, half on the bed. With that, I push all thoughts of Luke's stick out of my mind. The last thing I should be doing is thinking about what's between my best friend's legs.

"You know what I mean," I say.

"Actually, I don't."

I sigh. How do I explain this? "You're the best guy I know, Luke. And the *only* guy I trust, but—"

"Then maybe you should marry me," he teases as his hands go to my hips, and his big fingers biting into my skin.

I burst out laughing at that. "...but, I don't think of you as a *real* guy," I say putting emphasis on the word real.

"I could prove to you that I am a real guy."

"Stop it," I say, and whack him.

We both go quiet for a long time, then Luke breaks he silence. "You really want to go on my honeymoon?"

I put my chin on his chest and stare up at him. "Yeah, sure. I don't think I'll like skiing, but Italy..."

"If you're pretending be my wife, does that mean I get all the benefits that come with it?" He wags his brows in a suggestive manner, and I'm happy to see him back to his old playful self. "You did say we could find other ways to pass the time."

"Of course," I tease in return. "You get all the benefits."

"Really?" His eyes go wide, like he actually believes I might want sex with him. Jeez, I get that he was kidding. He doesn't need to be terrified of the idea.

"God no," I say. "Now let's get some sleep. Tomorrow we have to pack and get ready for our fake honeymoon." His breathing changes, becomes deeper, but before sleep overcomes him, I whisper, "Luke?"

"Yeah?" he asks, his voice groggy.

"You okay?"

His arms hold me a bit tighter. "Yeah, thanks for coming tonight."

"I'll always be here for you. You know that."

"I know that."

"That's why you love me."

"You think that's why I love you?" he says, and I smile at his familiar response as I close my eyes and drift off to sleep.

3

LUKE

"My God, I'm freezing my balls off," Katee says. I drag her closer to me as I fish the key to our chalet from my pocket. She wraps her arms around my waist and we use our body heat to stay warm. We're both from Texas, now living in Seattle. Neither one of us are acclimated to this kind of cold.

"You don't have balls, remember?" I say.

"Well if I did have balls, they'd be frozen."

"Yeah, mine are halfway there," I say, and she chuckles. Feigning offense, I ask, "You think that's funny?"

"No, not funny at all." She unsuccessfully tries to stifle a laugh. "Hurry so we can get inside and warm them up."

"We?"

"Well not we, but you."

Too bad because I can think of a few ways *we* can warm them up, and all the ways I can warm her up in return. The truth is my balls ache, are tight against my body, but it's not from the below freezing temperatures here in the mountains. No, it's because they ache to be touched by her soft hands, kissed by her warm mouth.

Okay, cool it, dude, this is your best friend, and she doesn't want you like that.

"Hurry up, Luke," she says, her teeth chattering so hard, I'm worried they're going to crack. Stepping back, she hops from one leg to the other, and rubs her hands together. "I'm going to Bali on my honeymoon."

My breath turns to fog in front of my face when I say, "I thought you said you weren't getting married."

"I'm not, but still…Bali."

I open the door and grab our suitcases. Katee rushes inside and I drop the bags and step up to her. Her nose is red, her lips an odd shade of blue. "I need to warm you up," I say, and pull her to me, running my hands over her body to create heat with friction. She snuggles closer, until I can feel every inch of her. Fire races through my veins, and the familiar tightness in my pants induces a yearning in me I know better than to act on. Dammit, maybe this wasn't such a great idea. Being here with her like this, sharing a chalet and pretending we're married is like a ticking time bomb. Sooner or later something is going to blow. And by something, I mean my cock, or our friendship. Since I refuse to let anything come between us—especially my feelings toward her—I plan to spend a great amount of time abusing myself in the shower.

"You probably should have worn more than yoga pants. They won't keep you warm in this kind of cold."

"Sooo…cold…" she chatters. The walk from the main lodge to our chalet wasn't far, but it's late in the day, the sun having gone down ages ago, and we're simply not used to these below zero temperatures.

"Let me get a fire going."

She stays cuddles in to me. "Don't let go."

I hold her a moment longer, rub my hands on her arm, think about how good we fit together. She lifts her chin, and her lips part slightly and it's all I can do not to claim her mouth, lose myself in her sweet taste. My entire body stiffens. Dammit, I need to stop thinking about her in my bed.

"There's a fully stocked bar. Why don't you pour us a drink, something to warm us up." Hopefully that will numb the things I'm feeling and help me get my head on right.

She reluctantly pulls away, and I step up to the fire. "It's propane." I flick a switch, and it lights up. "That was easy."

Katee grabs a bottle of brandy and pours two glasses. "Here." I take one from her, and we clink glasses. "What are we toasting too?" she asks.

"To best friends," I say. "Who are always there for each other." I leave out the part about one of them wanting to ravish the other. No need to send her to the hills screaming.

She nods in agreement, and with a flick of her wrist, drains the amber liquid with one easy swallow.

"Ohmigod," she yelps. "I...my throat."

I finish my drink, set our glasses on the mantel and reach for her. "Come here." I move her in front of the flames and she holds her hands out to warm them. We stay like that for a few minutes until her lips are no longer blue. "Better?" I ask.

She nods and I back up to shrug out of my jacket. She spins around, her gaze cataloguing the chalet. "My God, this is a lot nicer than I ever expected."

I follow her gaze, to take in the fully stocked kitchen, the bathroom, and patio, and the big bed in front of the fire. "I couldn't get the honeymoon suite," I say. "They were booked up."

"I don't need the honeymoon suite. All I need is this fire, and you, for a perfect getaway."

If only she needed me the way I needed her.

"Oh, and food, and maybe a bottle of wine or some beer," she adds. "Not high maintenance at all," she adds with a laugh. "That's why you love me."

"You think that's why I love you?" I say as I take in her rosy cheeks.

"Of course."

She's right, her easy-going attitude is one of the many things I love about her. She doesn't need designer clothes, makeup or fancy shoes and purses to make her happy. After her father left, she and her mother survived on very little, but she never once complained about her lot in life. Whenever I tried to buy her things, she got mad at me, insisted on paying her own way, or going without. She had no daddy to give her credit cards, and wouldn't in a million years think about going after a guy for his money. Why the hell is she still single anyway? Oh right, she has a deep distrust of guys.

I look at the big king-sized bed. "It only has one bed, though," I say.

She shrugs. "We've shared a bed before."

"True, but you can't expect me to sleep in that bed with my wife, and not have sex with her," I tease. Or maybe I'm not teasing. Jesus, I'm so fucked. "This *is* our honeymoon."

She elbows me in the gut and air leaves my lungs. "I am not your wife. I'm only pretending to be."

She leans to the side, one curvy hip jutting out as she gathers her long hair, and pulls an elastic off her wrist. It's a familiar move, one I've seen her do numerous times, but it's still as sexy as fuck. She throws herself onto the bed, grabs the remote and stretches out. "Think we can get any English stations?" she asks as she flicks on the TV.

"Probably, this place caters to tourists."

She flicks through the stations, and I head to the kitchen. The fridge is full of snack foods that I'd ordered in ahead of times. Most of our meals will be in the local restaurants. "Hungry?"

"Starving."

I search around, and pull out cream cheese, smoked

salmon, and grab some crackers from the cupboard. Arianna hates most of the things Katee and I like, and would never be caught dead eating carbs this late at night. Then again, for years now Katee has been watching what she eats. Not that she needs to. She's perfect no matter her size. Dropping the food onto the counter, I lift my gaze, find her peeling her coat from her body.

"Warming up?"

"Yes." She taps the bed, stretches out and widens her legs. "But you in this bed sharing your body heat, and food too, of course, will help me warm up even more."

Jesus, when she says stuff like that, it fills my head with inappropriate thoughts. I briefly pinch my eyes shut and work to get my shit together. Seriously though, does she not have any idea what sharing a bed with her does to me? How hard it is for me not to strip her bare and show her how could we could be together when she puts her hands on my body? How can she be so unaware of the effect she has on me?

Oh, because she doesn't think of you as a real guy, dude.

I guess that's why no matter how much I tease her, no matter how many inappropriate things I say it just rolls off her shoulders. Fuck, I want to tell her how I feel, but she's made it blatantly clear that she doesn't think of me as anything other than her friend. I can't risk telling her and making things awkward. It would only ruin what we have. But being with her like this...well, everything about it feels so damn right.

If only this was *our* honeymoon—a real one. Then again, everything about it is wrong, because this isn't where she'd want to be. If I said as much, she'd no doubt flee, and I'd lose the best friend I ever had. But how can I fucking go on pretending? I can never marry or love another woman, not when I can't get past Katee. That much is obvious.

Then go get her.

Wait, what?

If you love her so much, make her see you as a real guy. Show her what the two of you could have together.

I pause as some inner voice urges me to go after what I want. Should I? Should I pull out all the plays and get my best friend to look at me as more?

What if ruins our friendship and she runs the other way?

What if she doesn't?

Fuck knows, I'm miserable. Can't move forward, backward or upside down in life and will likely end up miserable and alone if I don't do something. As that thought runs around my brain and taunts me, I go back to the fridge and pull out one more item. Oysters.

"Hey Luke, I found a station with chick flicks."

"Great," I groan.

She laughs. "Come on, don't pretend you don't like them."

I plate the food, grab two beers from the fridge and step back into the main living area. The fire is now blazing, creating a warm blue glow in the cozy chalet. I hand her a beer, and set the plate on the bed between us. As I do I can't help but think of Ari. She'd never be caught eating in bed, let alone drinking beer. When it comes right down to it, she's the antithesis of Katee. Maybe that's why I went with it. Nothing about her reminded me of the girl I'm crazy about. Seriously though, did I really think that would help me move on?

When Katee sees all the food, she gives a deep, sexy moan that strokes my dick. "My favorites."

"I know. Mine too. I had the placed stocked for my honeymoon."

She gives me a disbelieving look. "Are you telling me Arianna eats cream cheese and crackers?"

"No, but you do, so I called in yesterday and added a few things to the list."

"Aww, you're so sweet. I probably shouldn't eat any of this, though."

I pick up a buttery cracker and put it in her mouth. Her eyes roll back. "You're perfect, I told you that. Now eat."

As she chews the cracker, she picks up an oyster and crinkles her nose. "Wait, Oysters? Since when did we start eating oysters?"

I wink at her. "It's our honeymoon. Helps with the mood."

Rolling her eyes at me, she slides one into her mouth. "Mmm...delish." Goddammit, that mouth. What I'd do to slide my cock in there, hear her moan around it. "Wait, I didn't just swallow a pearl, did I?"

I laugh at that. "Pretty sure you didn't."

"It would be cool to find a pearl in one, though, don't you think?"

"Chances are slim."

"Still, a girl can hope, and what fun it would be to open one and find a surprise inside." She licks her bottom lip, and to stop myself from leaning into her, and tasting her mouth, I glance at the TV. I read the little logo on the bottom right of the screen. "I'm not watching any station called Passionflix, unless it's porn."

Katee giggles and nudges me. "Remember that time we watched that dirty show when your mom and dad were out?"

I fix my pillow, settle against the headboard, and toss an oyster into my mouth. "I remember." Fuck, do I ever remember. It was the beginning of my porn addiction. One that led to many nights masturbating to the image of Katee.

"That was kind of fun," she says, reaching for a cracker. "Very educational."

I nearly choke on my oyster. "Educational?"

She shrugs and spreads cream cheese on a cracker. "I was

sixteen. I had never given a blow job before and had no idea what to experience in bed."

"I hope you're not basing your experiences now on what you saw then?"

She grimaces. "No, not really."

"Jesus, Katee." I sit up a little straighter. "You are, aren't you?"

She averts her gaze, nibbles her cracker. "Uh...no."

"Real life sex shouldn't be like what you see in porn. On the screen, it's usually wham, bam, thank you, ma'am." I hope to fuck the men she's been with have done right by her, putting her needs above their own, and cherishing her like she deserves. But as I think about that, rage prowls through my blood. I cannot, for one second, think about another man with his hands or mouth on her.

She blinks up at me. "I just...that's how I learned to give a proper blow job."

Kill me. Fucking. Now.

"You're telling me you give porn star blow jobs?"

She puts her hand over her mouth and giggles some more. "I don't know if I'd classify them as porn star blow jobs." She grabs her pillow and covers her face to hide her embarrassment. "I used to think you had to blow on a guy. Like actually blow on him." Her voice is muffled through the pillow and for a second I wonder if I heard her right. "I'm so glad we watched that movie. I would have made a complete fool out of myself."

As I try to dispel the image of another man's cock in her mouth, I take the pillow away. "You could have searched it on the internet to learn how it was done. Or asked me."

She gives a fast shake of her head, her brown eyes big and horrified. "My mother used to borrow my laptop. I couldn't risk her or anyone seeing what I was searching for, and I wasn't about to ask you."

"Why not?" Without thinking it through, I jump from the bed, fish my laptop out of my carry-on bag and settle down next to her, closer this time. I wait for her to answer my question, and when she doesn't, I continue with, "Did you at least learn about what physical things *you* liked in bed from watching porn?" Leave it to Katee to be concerned about a man's pleasure before her own.

She tosses another oyster into her mouth. "No. I learned that from touching myself." As soon as the words leave her mouth, she makes an 'eeping' sound, and grabs the pillow again. With my cock jumping in my pants, I pull it away, and my gaze rakes over her face. Jesus, she's so sexy when she blushes.

"Don't be shy with me," I say. "I'm not a *real* guy, remember." Shit, what am I doing? She's my best friend and she trusts me. I shouldn't be using our closeness to find out about her sex life. But there is a part of me that wants to make sure she's getting what she needs in the bedroom. Too bad the other part is the guy who wants to give it to you.

"I know, but we don't usually talk about sex." She wipes the corners of her mouth. "I think the oysters are loosening my tongue."

I hand her another one.

"What are you doing?" she asks when I pull up my favorite porn site.

"We're going to watch porn."

She sits up a little straighter. "We are?"

I give a casual shrug, even though nothing about this situation feels casual. "Sure, why not?"

"Ah, because...I'm not sixteen anymore."

"You're my best friend, and there are a lot of assholes out there. I just want to make sure your expectations are on target."

"Look, I get porn is just about the physical act, and it supposedly feels different when emotions are involved."

"Yeah, there's a difference," I say, even though I've never experienced it firsthand. "But I just want you to know that any guy who is with you should put you on a pedestal and treat you right in the bedroom. Even without the emotions, I need to make sure you know what 'treating you right' really means."

She whistles and gives a slow shake of her head. "My God, Arianna is one lucky woman."

My stomach drops. Fuck man, I wish I could tell Katee the truth. She deserves that from me, but I'm a guy of my word and I gave my word to Arianna. One week. One week of silence. After Ari comes to her senses and I make a clean break, I'll tell Katee everything.

Will you tell her how you feel?

I'm not sure, but until then, we'll watch a little porn, and ride out our week here, away from the public eye and the scrutiny. Ari is a beloved socialite, and I can just imagine the shit that's being said about me. But here on the slopes, I don't expect anyone to know me, so I can relax and enjoy the anonymity for a change. I hit the play button and move the near empty plate of food out of our way to be even closer to her. Our legs touch, and my entire body tenses. I silently curse under my breath. How the hell am I going to make it a week—a night—sharing this bed without putting my hands and mouth all over her?

She eyes me, and I hold my breath. Has she finally woken up, become aware of what her touch does to me? Is she going to call me out on that?

"Do you have a porn subscription or something?" she asks, and I let loose a relieved breath.

"Something like that," I say, and she grins at me.

She widens her legs, then closes them, like she's making

snow angels. "Here I thought I knew everything about you."

I grin at her. "You don't know everything, Katee."

"That seems like a challenge to me," she says playfully. "Maybe I'll have to spend the week figuring out all your dirty little secrets."

Oh, if she only knew.

The movie starts, and Katee shifts restlessly beside me as the opening credits roll. In all of ten seconds flat, we're watching an office romance porn—and I use the word *romance* lightly—where the boss wastes no time going down on his secretary on top of his desk. I chose this one on purpose, knowing exactly how it opened. I angle my head to see Katee, note the way her breathing has changed as she absently twirls her hair around her finger, something she does when she's concentrating. I'm not even sure she knows she's doing it. But I'm well aware of her body language, what she's saying without using her voice.

I turn back to the screen as the woman shamelessly rubs herself up against her boss. "Like what you see, Katee?"

"Yeah," she says, her voice a breathless whisper. "That's good," she says so quietly I have to strain to hear her. Okay, maybe this wasn't my smartest move because seeing my best friend aroused, admitting how she likes watching a guy go down on his girl, and not being able to do anything about it might just be the end of me.

Why can't you do anything about it?

"So...uh...you've done this, right?" I ask.

She slowly turns her head my way, her eyes a bit glazed. "I've never *done* that, but I've been on the receiving end of it, if that's what you're asking."

I clear my throat. "That's what I'm asking, and good. Every woman should get off on oral sex before penetration. That's rule number one in my playbook, and I just want to make sure it is in yours, too."

She goes quiet for a moment, and looks back at the screen. "Luke?"

"Hmm?" I hit the volume on the keyboard, turn it down a bit to hear her whispered words.

"I've never really..." She points to my laptop, and crinkles up her cute little nose. "Orgasmed from that, though."

I scrub my chin, as the visual of her sprawled across a desk—or this bed—my face buried between her legs until she comes all over my tongue fill my thoughts. "Shit."

"Why shit?" A worried look comes over her face and she shuffles backward like she's just been slapped. What the hell? What is going on with her?

"No...nothing, uh. Wait, you do you enjoy oral sex, don't you?" She gives a nonchalant shrug.

"It's...okay. I guess."

"Just okay?" I briefly close my eyes. I'm starting to get the sense that no guy has ever done it right for her?

"I wouldn't write home about it or anything."

"And I'm sure you mother appreciates that," I say and we both laugh, the tension easing a bit between us. I watch the guy lick the girl's sex, circle her clit, and I shift the laptop to hide my erection. A frown comes over Katee, and I can't quiet figure out what it is about this scene that is both arousing her and bothering her. "What?"

"I...never mind." She looks down at the bedding.

"Spill. I'm your best friend, you can tell me anything."

"I just... I wonder if there is something wrong with me."

"How so?"

"You said a woman should get off on oral sex before penetration, right?"

"Yeah."

"I...ugh, this is so embarrassing."

I capture her hand, give it a squeeze. "Come on, since when were you not able to tell me something embarrassing."

"This is different."

"Different than the night you threw up in your hair and I had to put you in the shower." The flu had come upon her fast, and I had to strip her to her underwear and climb into the shower with her to get her clean. "What about the night you peed your pants because you drank too many energy drinks at the outdoor concert, and the line up to the bathrooms were a mile long." She groans, and I continue with, "How about the night—"

She puts her hand up, palm out. "Fine, fine. I don't need to be reminded of every screw up." She sets her beer on the nightstand, and watches the screen a moment longer before finally saying, "I think there is something wrong with my body." A loud moan from my computer speaker fills the room, and we both watch as the guy inserts his fingers into the girl's pussy, and she belts out a cry. Overacting much? "The only time I orgasm is when I touch myself. No guy has ever been able to do it for me. I think there's something wrong with me."

I nearly swallow my tongue as I visualize her hands on her body.

I take a deep breath, let it out slowly and hope I don't sound like I'd just eaten a bucket of nails when I ask, "So you're telling me no guy has really satisfied you? Has never taken the time to learn your body, learn your likes and dislikes?"

"I guess not."

Okay, Luke, here's your chance to change her view of you, and get her to see you as more. If what I have in mind doesn't change the way she looks at me, and she just thinks I'm helping her out, I have less of a chance of ruining our friendship.

Here goes nothing.

"Have you ever told a guy what you liked?"

She shakes her head. "God, no."

"Why not?"

"I don't know, Luke. I guess I just don't know how to say all the dirty things I'm thinking."

She thinks dirty things?

"Then do you show him?" I ask.

"Show him?

"You know, when he does something you like, you moan in response, or you know...grab his head and hold him between your legs when he's licking you just right."

She takes in a fast breath. "Ah, no, not really."

"Look, Katee, there is nothing wrong with you. You just need to give a few nonverbal clues if you're not comfortable saying what you like." I tap my head. "We catch on quick. We're not all thick up here."

She reaches for her beer and takes a big drink as the characters on screen shift positions.

"Nonverbal clues huh?"

My heart beats a little faster as the girl on screen takes the man's cock in her throat, giving him her best porn star blowjob. "We can practice, if you like," I suggest. "I can teach you how to show a man what you need in bed. I can show you how good it can really be."

She rolls her eyes, and whacks my stomach. "Yeah, right."

I grab her hand, hold it in mine, until her gaze flicks my way. "I'm serious, Katee."

"What...what about Ari?"

"We're over," I say bluntly

"I'm sure it's just temporary—"

"I'm a free man. I can do anything I want, and what I want is to show you what to expect in bed."

She blinks once, twice, the smile falling from her sweet mouth. "Really?"

"Yeah. What are friends for, right?"

KATEE

OMG. OMG. OMG.

One minute I'm watching porn with my best friend, the next I'm in the shower alone, staying under the needle-like spray, and gobbling up all the hot water until it's icy. I can't believe for one second Luke is suggesting we sleep together. At first I didn't think he was serious. Then when I realized he was, I bolted to the bathroom like I was being chased by demons, saying I needed to shower after a long day of traveling—and that I would think about it.

Am I really going to think about it?

Luke wants to help me out in the bedroom? Teach me how to show a guy what I like, how good sex really can be?

Okay, apparently, I am going to think about it.

What the fuck is going on, and why on earth would he suggest that? Oh, maybe because I admitted my shortcomings to him, confessed my fears and he's just trying to be a good friend and prove there is nothing wrong with me. But what about Arianna? Would that be considered cheating on her? I'm not a homewrecker, and wouldn't do anything to come between my best friend and his fiancée.

Ex fiancée.

Right! I guess technically they're not a couple anymore. As I consider that, I slide my hand between my legs, feel the dampness that has nothing to do with the tepid water pouring over me. I hadn't watched porn in years, and I'd be lying if I said it didn't arouse me. Heck, maybe I should take him up on his offer, let him take care of my needs while teaching me a thing or two about how to get what I want between the sheets. Lord knows I'd love for sex to be better than it has been. Once, just once, I want a man to touch me the way I need to be touched, to bring me to heavenly bliss, so I don't have to do it myself once the night is over.

I stroke my clit lightly, and my entire body trembles as I consider sleeping with Luke. But he's my best friend, has always treated me like one of the guys, and sex between us would be weird, right?

Or would it?

Wait, what the hell am I thinking? I'm not about to have sex and risk ruining what we have. Besides, why is he thinking about having sex with me in the first place, when he's waiting for his fiancée to come to her senses and carry on with the wedding?

Unless...he's not.

Oh, cut it out, Katee. Of course he is, and thinking he's not, is just wishful thinking on your part.

Wishful thinking?

No. No. No.

I don't want Luke like that. Never have and never will.

I turn the shower off, grab a big fluffy towel and wrap it around myself. I look at my pile of clothes on the floor. In my hurry to get away from him, I forgot to grab something clean to wear. I inch open the door, search the room, and find Luke on the bed exactly where I left him. I'm about to call out to him, but stop. I crack the door a bit more, let my gaze rake over his body as his fingers race over the keyboard on his laptop, which in now on the bed beside him. Is he still watching porn, or searching for something else, something more appropriate for best friends to watch? My gaze searches his handsome face, takes in the intensity in his dark eyes before my eyes travel downward, to examine his broad shoulders and...omg...huge bulge in his pants. The man is seriously turned on.

He's not the only one.

I clear my throat to gain his attention. "Hey Luke, can you grab me my pajamas. There in my bag." I tug the towel around myself tighter, and the hiss of my suitcase zipper reaches my ear as he searches through it. A moment later, he sticks his hand through the door and I snatch my bra and panties from him. Dammit why didn't he grab me a shirt or something. Oh, probably because he knows I wear next to nothing to bed. I can't stand to have clothes bunching up around me when I sleep.

I hurry into them, brush my teeth and comb out my hair, my entire body on hyperdrive. My hand shakes slightly as I reach for the door. I pull it open, working to pretend nothing is out of the ordinary, when in fact everything is out of whack. Not to mention my body. It's completely and utterly off kilter. How can it not be? I mean my best friend just offered to have sex with me. Is there any coming back from that? I sure as hell hope so, because I wouldn't want it to come between us, make this week awkward. The warmth of the place hits me like a slap as I cross the room. Luke is no longer on the bed. I scan the chalet and find him in the kitchen, dressed in nothing but a pair of jeans.

Lord have mercy.

For the first time in my life, I'm looking at him differently. Okay, maybe that's not entirely true. Maybe, just maybe, there was a small part of me that imagined what it would be like to be in bed with him. But I shut those thoughts down as fast as they came because friends don't fantasize about each other, right? Not that Luke is fantasizing about me. I'm not a total idiot. He's just looking to help me out. The same way I'm here on his honeymoon with him, helping him out. Maybe he just wants to do something nice for me as thanks.

His eyes slowly lift to mine, and I don't miss the heat in his gaze as they travel the length of my body. He's seen me in my underwear hundreds of times. Heck he's even seen me naked, but never, ever in my life has he looked at me with such hunger. A reaction to watching porn, no doubt.

Working to appear casual—even though everything about this situation is messed up—I walk across the room. But it's suddenly difficult to put one foot in front of the other. I'm conscious of my every movement, the intensity in Luke's gaze. I struggle to keep things light as I tear my gaze from his chest, and glance at the television above the fire. Passionflix is still playing.

"Want me to change the station?" I ask. Holy shit, is that my voice.

"Whatever you want to watch." He turns his back to me and sets the dishes in the sink. "I'm easy." My gaze drops to his perfect ass, and a whimper I have no control over catches in my throat. He turns but I'm far too slow to react, and when he catches me blatantly checking him out, a small smile curls his mouth.

"Like what you see?" he asks again, but this time he's talking about his body and not the porn.

Okay yeah. Of course, I like what I see. How could I not? I've always admired his body, but now I'm suddenly looking at it differently. I consider his question. If I say yes, there's a good chance I'll end up in the bed beneath him. If I say no, it might make things awkward between us.

Not knowing which way to turn, my gaze flickers to his

closed laptop—like my answer is to watch more porn—then flies back to him. That small smirk is still turning up the corner of his mouth.

He dries his hands and comes back into the room. "I think I'll take a shower," he says and peels off his jeans. I quickly avert my gaze as he kicks them away. Lacking any sort of modesty, he walks into the bathroom.

"I think I used all the hot water," I squeak out as warmth prowls through my body at his near nakedness.

"That's good. I should probably take a cold shower, anyway." Before he shuts the door, my eyes drop, settle on the large bulge in his boxers. My mouth instantly waters. I've never really loved giving oral sex before, so for the life of me I can't quite figure out why I'm dying to put his cock in my mouth.

A strange strangled noise crawls out of my throat and I race across the room, jump under the covers and pull a pillow over my head. The water turns on and I stifle a chuckle when Luke yelps. I really did gobble up the hot water. But that chuckle turns to a moan as I visualize him naked in that shower, his hand all over his body...his cock. I shift restlessly, and put my hand between my legs. If I said yes, I could be the one in there soaping and touching his body.

Is that what you want, Katee?

A little moan rises in my throat and I slide my hand into my panties, lightly stroke myself. My clit pulses in my hand, and I'm pretty sure I've never been more turned on in my life. I close my eyes, and stroke myself, all the while imagining it's Luke between my legs.

I'm imagining Luke is between my legs?

I jackknife up, and my breath comes in ragged bursts when he comes from the shower in nothing but a big white towel that does little to hide his erection. He walks to his suitcase, and drops the towel, giving me an unobstructed view of his perfect backside as he bends to grab a pair of boxers. He tugs them on, and flicks off the lights as he slides in next to me.

"So Passionflix, huh?" he says as I stare at the TV.

I twirl my hair around my finger. "Yeah, it's a station that showcases all romance movies."

"For a girl who doesn't believe in love and marriage, you're kind of a romantic at heart."

"Yeah, except romances aren't like what we see on the screen," I say and wave toward the TV, "It's not like that in real life, Luke."

He gives a non-committal shrug. "Maybe it's better in real life."

"Like your porn and sex?"

Okay, Katee, why are you bringing the conversation back to sex?

Oh, because maybe I really want it.

He grins at me. "Take your time, Katee. Think about what I said. There's no rush. We have all week."

As I listen to his raspy voice, revel in the way it scrapes over my flesh, my nipples harden. I tug the blankets up tighter, to hide my body's reaction. Oddly enough, things already feel different between us, and I hate that. I don't want to lose what we have. I *can't* lose what we have. Just then another thought hits.

Maybe we have to have sex to save the relationship.

How is that for logical thinking at its worst?

LUKE

Last night I tugged one out in a cold shower, but that did little to diminish my need for the beautiful woman sound asleep beside me. Jesus fuck, I want her. In so many goddamn ways it's making my head spin. After my offer to help her out in bed, I noticed the way she started looking at me. Like I *was* a real guy. Yeah, okay, I get it. What I'm doing is risky. I can't ruin what we have, but I have to take a chance with her, otherwise I'm going to go fucking insane.

In the end, if I fail at what I'm doing—and she doesn't want more—I can simply assure her I was just helping out a friend, and nothing more. Sure, I'll be miserable for the rest of my life, but isn't that better than a life without her in it?

I swallow down a groan as my gaze slides the length of her body. With her blankets kicked to the bottom of the bed—she does have a tendency to thrash around in the night—I'm gifted with a view of her near nakedness. Jesus how I'd love to slip those lacy panties from her hips, put her legs around my neck and bury my face in her sweet sex. I take a deep breath and pull the sweet scent of her skin into my lungs.

"Ah, good morning," she says, and reaches for the blankets to pull them up. My gaze flies to hers. Never before has she covered herself up in front of me. Then again, I've never blatantly ogled her before, either. Still, I can't let things get awkward between us.

Trying for casual, I push from the bed and head to the kitchen. "Didn't mean to wake you."

"You didn't. I was half awake."

"Sleep okay?"

"Not really," she says honestly, then hurries out with, "Probably all the traveling yesterday." She taps the mattress. "And the first night in a strange bed always messes me up."

Teasing her I say, "Oh, you sleep in many strange beds?"

"Numerous," she says. "I'm the queen puck bunny, remember?"

"Liar."

She tosses a pillow at me. "Why did you ask if you already knew the answer?"

I open and close the cupboards. "I need coffee."

"Me too." As if she suddenly forgot that I'd been mentally undressing her only seconds before, she jumps from the bed and helps me search. I reach over her, grabbing the grounds from the upper shelf. It's a position we've found ourselves in numerous times, but today, the electricity arcing between us is enough to power the gondola for a week straight.

"I'll fill the carafe," she says and ducks out from beneath my arm. "You think the water from the tap is good to drink?"

"I'm sure it's fine, but there is bottled water in the fridge if you want it."

"You know how I feel about bottled water."

"I know. I know." I roll my eyes at her even though I totally agree we shouldn't be using bottled water, but Ari drinks only Fiji water, so we had it stocked. "We need to protect that planet."

She glares at me. "Are you saying we don't?" Before I can answer, she pinches my side, a pleasant reprieve from my nipple, which is what she usually abuses when she's pissed at me, or trying to make a point about something.

I flinch. "Jesus, that hurts."

"It's because you have no fat on your body."

I turn to her, wait for her to fill the carafe with tap water, then pinch her side. "Hey, that hurts." She swats my hands away. "What'd you do that for?"

"Why do you get to pinch, and I don't?" I challenge

She bobs her head. "Oh, is that how it's going to be?"

"Yeah, it's exactly how it's going to be. For the rest of this week, what you to do to me, I get to do to you in return."

Pink creeps into her cheeks, and I put my hands on either side of her, pinning her against the counter.

She angles her head, draws her bottom lip between her teeth. I can almost hear her mind racking. "Are we still talking about—"

I move closer, and lacking any sort of modesty, push my early morning arousal against her. "I'm talking about everything, Katee."

"Oh," she says, and her eyes leave mine to travel down my body. "So you're saying if I pinch you here," She pauses and rolls her finger around my nipple.

"Then I get to do the same to you," I say. "Tit for tat."

Her eyes go big. "I'm not sure I'd like for you to pinch my nipple." Her words say one thing but there is a breathless quality to her voice that might suggest otherwise.

"How do you know?"

She opens her mouth like she's about to say something, then closes it again. Her brow furrows. "I guess I don't."

I make a tsking sound. "Katee, I have so much to teach you." I cup her chin and lift it until her eyes meet mine. "All you have to do is say the word and we can get started."

Her eyes darken, a storm brewing in their shadowy depths. She opens her mouth, but I put my finger to her lips. "Not yet," I say. "We actually have ski lessons planned this morning. Part of the package."

Yeah, I could suggest we skip them, and spend the day in bed, but I'd prefer to build the anticipation between us. Let her think about all the things we can do to each other in that bed, let her warm to the idea. When she finally comes to me, I want her ready, willing, and quivering with need.

"I can't ski." Her voice is so low, a breathless whisper, I have to strain to hear it.

"That's why we're having ski lessons," I tease.

She glares at me again, and is two seconds from pinching my nipple when she catches herself. "Oh."

"Yeah, oh," I say. "Why don't you get dressed? The coffee will be ready when you finish, then we'll grab breakfast at Pasticceria Alvera," I say with a botched Italian accent. "I hear they have the best breakfast pastries."

Her mouth drops open. "You want me to eat cake for breakfast?"

"Sure, why not? We're on our honeymoon."

She plants one hand on her hip. "I am not eating sweets for breakfast. I...I won't fit into my pants by the end of the week."

"Pants are overrated." I shrug. "But if you're worried, there are ways we can work that off."

"I...you...ugh." Flustered, she storms from the kitchen and I chuckle as I finish the coffee. The shower turns on and I inch open her door. "If you plan to take all the hot water, let me know now, and I'll jump in there with you so we can conserve."

"Very funny," she says.

"Wasn't trying to be funny. I nearly froze my balls off last night."

Her chuckle reaches my ear and I grin. "Save me a tiny bit, okay?"

I go back to the kitchen and when the shower turns off, I fix her coffee. She comes out in nothing but a towel and roots through her suitcase. Jesus, does she always have to stick her ass in the air like that when she bends over.

I walk over to her and hand her a cup of coffee. She takes a sip and briefly closes her eyes. "Thanks." Her lids open. "There should be plenty of hot water," she says as she takes another sip.

"Aww, look at you." I wink at her. "All worried about my balls."

She chokes on her coffee, and spits it all over me. "Ohmigod Luke, don't make me laugh when I have a mouth full."

A mouth full.

Oh, fuck, now all I can visualize is my best friend with a mouth full of my cock. Giving me a porn star blow job. My dick grows another inch.

Coffee drips down my chest and she grabs a paper towel and starts blotting it against my skin. Her fingers brush my flesh and I groan, letting her blatantly know when her touch is doing to me.

"You should jump in the shower," she says as she pulls her hand back.

"Yeah, good plan." I head to the bathroom and don't bother shutting the door tight behind me. I rarely do. Katee is welcome to come in any time she likes. I turn on the spray and climb under, letting the warm water fall over me. I grab the soap and as I wash myself, my dick twitches. I grip the base of my cock, and give a good hard stroke, all the while visualizing it's Katee's hands on my body. A groan crawls out of my throat.

"You okay in there?" Katee asks.

"Yeah, I'll be right out." I wash quickly, shampoo my hair, and turn off the spray. The air is cool against my hot skin as I climb out, and knot a towel around my waist. I step into the room and Katee is pulling the blankets up on the bed, her sweet ass aimed my way. Fuck, what I'd give to pull her pants down, lay her out on the bed and put my cock all the way inside her. Another groan catches in my throat and she turns to me.

"You sure you're okay. You sound like you're in agony."

"I am," I say, and her gaze drops to the bulge in my towel.

"Were you watching porn in there or something?" She turns and fusses with the pillows. When she finishes, there is a pretty pink blush on her face.

I drop my towel and she gives a little gasp as I reach into my suitcase. "You've seen me naked before, Katee," I say casually. "Touched almost every inch of me. No need to be embarrassed now."

"Yeah, but that was before..."

"Before what?"

"Before you suggested we have sex. Now, well. Now I can't seem to look at your body the same way."

"So you think I'm a real guy now, Katee?"

"Yeah, definitely, and then some."

I chuckle at that, tug on my clothes, and rake my hand through my hair to comb it.

"You can't go out with your hair wet like that," she says. "Hang on." She run to the bathroom and comes back with a hair dryer. "Sit here."

I flop into one of the chairs and she runs her fingers through my hair as she turns on the blower. Fuck, I love how she touches me. I put my hand around the chair and grip her leg, needing my hands on her, anywhere. She finishes my hair, and I stand.

"Thanks." I scrub the top of my head. "It's so short."

"That's because you got yourself all cleaned up for your wedding." As soon as the words leave her mouth, her eyes go wide. "I...ah..." she begins, like she's trying to retract.

"It's okay—"

"In one week, everything will be fine, I'm sure of it," she says quickly.

"I hope so." Fuck man, I pray to fucking God that Ari comes to her senses and realizes what a colossal mistake it would be for us to get married.

"We should go." Katee averts her gaze as she grabs our coats, handing mine to me.

"You ready for this?" I ask.

"As ready as I'll ever be. But you do know I'll probably break my damn neck, right?"

I grab her zipper and pull it to her chin. Then adjust her hat on her head. "You want to sit this one out?"

"No, I'm game."

I give her a grin, and nudge her chin with my fist. "That's my Katee. Always such a good sport."

She angles her chin up. "That's what you love about me."

"Oh, you think that's what I love about you," I say, and open the door. A gust of wind whips over us and Katee shivers.

"I guess if I don't break my neck, I'll freeze to death. Either way, here goes nothing," she says and steps outside.

I lock up behind us, and put my arm around her to keep her warm as we head to breakfast. We enter the restaurant and Katee moans.

"Ohmigod, Luke. This place smells divine." We step up to the counter, and Katee's eyes practically glaze over as she takes in all the breakfast sweets.

More people pile in behind us. "The place is packed. Why don't you find us a table, and I'll grab us something."

She nods and peels off her coat as she moves through the

crowd. I put an order in for two coffees and crepes, as well as a pastry with sugar-coated raspberries on it. I pay for the food, and make my way through the crowd to find Katee. She's sitting at a table with another couple, which takes me by surprise.

"Hey," I say and take my coat off. I put it over my chair and sit.

"Luke, this is Becca and Trey. They saw me searching and offered us their table. They're here on their honeymoon too. They're both from Canada."

Trey's mouth drops open as he looks at me. "Wait, aren't you—"

Shit, I never expected anyone to know me, but Canadians do love their hockey. I shake the guy's hand. "Yes, and it's nice to meet you Trey."

"How long have you been here?" Becca asks, before she takes a sip of her coffee.

"We just got in yesterday," Katee answers. Becca smiles at us, and leans in to her husband. "Same," she says. "Did you guys sign up for the honeymoon package?"

"We did," I say, when Katee looks at me. I take her hand in mine and bring it to my lips.

"I guess we'll see you tonight for the sleigh ride and bonfire, then?" Trey says.

"It's on the agenda."

"Although I might not make it," Katee says.

"Ooh," Becca teases. "Busy doing other things?"

"Well, yes, but no." Katee crinkles her nose. "I'm probably going to break my neck on the hill today."

"You don't like skiing?" Becca asks.

"My first time."

"Then why—"

"I should have taken her to Bali," I say, and everyone

laughs. Just then, our food arrives. The waitress sets our plates down, and clears Becca and Trey's away.

"We'll let you eat." They both stand and grab their coats from the back of their chairs. "See you tonight," Trey says.

"Cute couple," Katee says after they leave.

"Not as cute as we are."

She grins and looks at the food in front of her. "Raspberry tart. Luke, you're killing me." She takes a big bite and moans.

"You don't have to eat it."

"Yeah, I do," she says and lets her eyes drift shut. I chuckle. "At least you'll still love me when I'm two hundred pounds heavier at the end of the week.

"You're perfect, Katee. You've always been perfect."

She grins. "You have to say that. You're my *husband*."

"I'm saying it because it's true."

Ignoring that, she takes another bite and moans. "So what comes with this honeymoon package you booked?" she asks.

"Typical honeymoon things."

She angels her head. "How am I supposed to know what typical honeymoon things are? This is my first honeymoon, you know."

"Mine too," I say and she frowns. "What?"

Her hand closes over mine. "I'm sorry, Luke. I get that this situation is all messed up, and things aren't the way they're supposed to be."

"You're right, they're not."

KATEE

Even though I'm dressed in a big ski jacket, with hat, gloves and boots, the cold still manages to seep into my bones. Luke puts his arm around me and drags me to him as we make our way to the lodge for our honeymoon sleigh ride, followed by a bonfire.

The slopes are lit up, people taking full advantage of the nighttime skiing. I snuggle in closer to Luke, and when he rubs his hand up and down my arm, something he's done a million times before, the way my body awakens doesn't go unnoticed. I've always been aware of him, but ever since he offered to help me out in the bedroom, I've not been able to look at him without thinking of sex. A needy shiver goes through me and he mistakes it for cold.

"What am I going to do to get you warm?" he asks

My mind instantly drifts, imagining his hard body on mine, warming me with his mouth as he kisses a path down my body. I shiver again, and angle my head to see him. There is a small grin curling up the corner of his mouth, and I get the sense he knows what I've been thinking. I haven't answered him yet. This morning, when he said all I had to do was say the word, I was all prepared to answer. Only problem was, I had no idea what word was going to come out of my mouth.

"Hey, you made it."

I glance up to see Becca waving us over to the group. From what I can tell, there are eight couples in total. When we reach our new friends, Becca looks me over. "No broken neck," she says.

"There were a few close calls," I say and laugh. "Actually, it was kind of fun. Though I'm not so sure I want to do it again."

"We didn't get off the bunny hill," Luke says, and Becca and Trey laugh. I glance around at all the other couples, many who are snuggled close. "Then again, we didn't come here to ski," Luke says, and presses his lips to mine. At first the kiss surprises me—since when has Luke been into public displays of affection?—but when his tongue slides along my bottom lip, I sink in to him. I've kissed Luke before. But never, ever like this. Holy hell, what is he doing to me, and how come I like it so much? His hands slide around my body, and he deepens the kiss as he holds me to him.

The sound of sleigh bells reaches our ears, and Luke breaks the kiss. I inch back and Becca and Trey are grinning.

"Sorry," Luke says. "I can't seem to keep my hands off my beautiful bride."

"I totally understand," Trey says, as he pulls Becca close. "I feel the same."

Becca hits him playfully, and I lean into Luke, go up on my toes and put my mouth to his ear. "What the hell was that?"

"Just playing the part," he says. "Letting you try it on for size since you're so anti-marriage." He nudges me. "Not so bad, right?"

Not so bad?

Jesus, if he can kiss like that, what the hell would it be like to actually sleep with him on a regular basis? I'm not sure, but now, well, I'm a little more anxious to find out.

The horses and sleigh pull up in front of us, and the driver steps down. "Welcome everyone," he says. He's a jovial man, probably in his late fifties, dressed in a big red jacket and black boots. He almost looks like Santa Claus. "Tonight we're going on a romantic sleigh ride around the village, and I'll be dropping you all off at the main lodge for a bonfire and games."

"Games?" someone in the group says.

He gives us a wink. "Let's just say there will be fabulous prizes for the couple who knows each other best."

I turn to Luke. "I want to win."

He laughs. "Me too."

I laugh with him. Neither of us know what the prize is, but we both have such a competitive nature.

"Now if you'll all climb aboard." Luke helps me onto the sleigh. I lower myself onto a pile of hay, and Luke sits on one side of me, while Becca and Trey settle in on the other. Once everyone is on board, the driver takes his seat and sets the horses in to motion.

"This is kind of fun," I say, and rub my hands together to keep warm. We head down a snowy path, and I take in all the lights. I know I'm not the girl he wants here with him, and I feel a little guilty that I'm glad it's me and not Arianna. She doesn't deserve Luke after what she'd done. I mull that over for a second, then quickly remind myself she is what *he* wants. Little bells on the rein jingles and pulls me back to the present. Around me everyone relaxes as they take in the majestic sights. Luke's thigh presses against mine, and I shimmy closer to absorb his heat.

The horses circle the icy lake, where families are skating

and laughing and drinking hot chocolate. "That looks like fun."

"We can do that tomorrow if you want."

"I'm way better on skates than skies," I say.

"Me too."

"You should be, you are the Stick Handler."

He leans in to me and his breath is warm on my ear when he whispers, "You think that's how I got the nickname."

I go still for a moment, then when he chuckles, the vibrations going right through me, I whack him. "Ohmigod, Luke. Spare me the details."

He laughs again. "I'd rather show you."

I turn to him, and beneath the stars I catch the lust in his eyes. It burns through my blood and as arousal takes hold, my nipples harden, and my panties grow damp.

Luke might have offered to teach me about sex—a friend helping a friend—but from everything he's said to me since we've been here, to the way he's looking at me right now, it's clear he wants everything that comes with this pretend honeymoon.

What do you want, Katee?

A big fat snowflake lands on my eyelash and I blink it away. "It's snowing," I squeal and open my mouth to catch a few falling flakes.

Becca laughs. "I take it you haven't seen a lot of snow in your lifetime."

"Not too much. Which is why I'm freezing to death here."

"The bonfire will warm us all up."

Luke puts his mouth back to my ear. "I'll warm you up."

Becca grins at me, and I wonder if she heard Luke. "I hope they have marshmallows," she says, and while I love marshmallows, I know better than to eat them, especially after this morning's tart.

We travel along the path for a little while longer, and eventually the driver stops in front of a gorgeous log lodge. The smell of a wood burning fire reaches my nose and I breathe it in.

"Okay folks," the driver says. "Everyone off. I'll be by in a couple of hours to take you all back to your lodging."

Luke jumps down, grips my waist and hauls me off. I slide down his body, and the groan in the back of his throat curls through me. He grips my hand and we walk into the lodge together. I spin to take it all in. It's elegant, yet rustic, and so damn cozy. In the middle of the room there is a huge walk-around fireplace, and there are trays of sandwiches, sweets, and marshmallows for roasting, set out for us.

"Wine or beer?" Luke asks, when he spots the bar.

"I'll have white wine."

He glances past my shoulder, and I take in his handsome face, specifically his beautiful lips.

I want them on my body.

"How about you, Becca and Trey?" Luke asks. "What can I get you?"

"I'll go with you," Trey says, and Becca reaches for my hand when we're alone.

"That man can't keep his hands off you," she teases.

I spin, and watch Luke walk away. My gaze drops to his ass, and a fine shiver moves through me.

"He's a hands-on kind of guy," I say.

"Trey is a huge fan of his. He told me they call him the Stick Handler." She giggles and says, "That sounds kind of dirty."

I laugh with her, my mind rewinding to what he said about his nickname. "You're right, it does, and I'm pretty sure he didn't get it from the ice."

"Then you're a damn lucky girl."

Not yet, but I could be.

"What are you two laughing about?" Trey asks, when the guys return.

"Girl stuff," I say and give Becca a wink.

Just then a middle-aged woman dressed in a wool sweater and jeans, her short hair tucked behind her ears, steps up to us all. "Welcome everyone. Please help yourself to some food, and grab a seat by the fire to warm up." She checks her watch. "My name is Veronica, and I'll be leading the games. We'll get going in a few minutes."

I hand my wine back to Luke as I shrug out of my coat. Then I take his drink so he can do the same. We all grab chairs near the fire and the warmth rushes over my body. I take another sip of wine, and I'm already starting to feel the effects. I lean into Luke, and he puts his arm around me.

"Okay folks, let's find out just how well you newlyweds really know each other."

Cheers erupt as she hands out sheets of paper attached to a clipboard and pencils to all the women. "What the heck are they going to make us do?" I ask.

"Beats me," Luke says. "As long as you don't have to draw, we'll be okay."

"Hey," I say and whack him. "I'm not that bad." Okay, I *am* that bad and Luke damn well knows it.

"How this game works is I'm going to ask some questions and the women will write their answer on the paper. Do not let your spouse see it." She waves her hand toward a back table. "We have a prize for everyone, and one grand prize to the last remaining couple."

I set my drink on the small table beside me, and wag my brows at Luke. "We got this."

"Okay, first question," Veronica begins. "What's the one thing your guy would save in a fire, besides you?"

I grin at Luke, and scribble my answer on the paper. Once we're done, Veronica begins to go around the room. "Couple number one," she says to the guy and girl at the end of the row, and points to the guy. "What's your answer?"

"My old baseball cards," he says, and his spouse smiles and holds up her sheet of paper, which says, baseball cards. Everyone claps, and the pair kiss each other. She goes around the room, polling all the couples, and some of the answers are hilarious.

When she gets to Luke, he says, "My hockey stick."

"Yay," I say, and hold up my paper, which says hockey stick. I nudge him. "Too easy."

Only one couple gets eliminated and they are given a gift bag with prizes in it.

"Now hand the clipboard and pen to the guys." Papers shuffle for a moment, then she begins again. "Okay, ladies, what was the first movie you ever saw together."

"Oh, shit," Luke says, and I whack him.

"You know this." He makes a face like he doesn't, and I swear if he gets it wrong, I'll pinch his...oh, wait. No, I won't pinch his nipple, otherwise he'll pinch mine and that would be...horrible...painful.... Fun?

Oh, God.

I suck in a fast breath, and Luke's eyes narrow in on me. "You okay?"

"Yeah," I say breathlessly. "Good."

He writes his answer down and Veronica goes around the room again. When she gets to me, I say, "The Lion King." Luke grins and holds up the answer. The Lion King.

"Really?" Becca asks.

"Luke and I've been best friends since kindergarten," I say, and she makes an aww sound.

With two more couples eliminated, there are only five couples left. We play a little more, and we answer questions, such as what's his most annoying habit, or her favorite body part. How he knew my favorite part on a guy was his ass is beyond me. Then again maybe it's just Luke's ass that always draws my attention and he had caught me staring at it a time or two. But dammit, the guy looks pretty damn good in his low-slung jeans.

"Okay, last question," Veronica says when it's only Luke, me, Becca and Trey left. She picks the card up and her eyes go wide. "Oh, this is a good one. Okay, how does your guy like to fall asleep. Cuddling, or apart?"

My mind goes back to all the times we fell asleep, most with me laying over him and listening to his strong heartbeat as he holds me close. I quickly write cuddling.

"Okay guys, what's the answer. Both men answer cuddling, and Becca and I laugh as we hold up our answers.

"I think I'm going to have to find a hard one," Veronica says. She grabs another card. "Okay, how about this. "What is your wife's favorite saying, and what is your response?" Luke scribbles something on his paper, and takes a pull from his beer bottle. He seems to be quite pleased with himself.

"Okay, ladies, what's the answer?"

Becca goes first and says, "I'm always saying, what goes around comes around, and Trey always responds with that's karma."

Trey groans and holds up his card, which says, "If it ain't broke, don't fix it, and I always say, it ain't broke because you didn't touch it."

Becca smacks her hand to her forehead, and laughs. "You're right, I do say that a lot, and that's how you respond."

As the two laugh and kiss, Veronica turns to us. "Okay, for the big prize package which consists of an upgrade to the presidential suite overlooking the ski hill, a helicopter ride, a couples massage at Serenity Spa and a romantic, candlelit rooftop dinner for two, what's your answer."

"That's why you love me, is something I say a lot, and Luke responds with, you think that's why I love you," I say.

Luke, catching me by surprise, leans in and plants a kiss right on my mouth. Honest to God, all this public display of affection is so unlike him. He might be a superstar hockey player, but underneath it all he's a private guy who likes to keep his private life...private. I'm sure it devastated him when Kari splashed his business all over social media.

I'm a bit breathless when he pulls back and shows me his answer, which was exactly what I said. He lowers his voice to say, "And tonight in the presidential suite, right after you answer me, we're going to do a whole lot of loving."

7

LUKE

I tip the concierge and thank him for bringing our luggage up. As soon as he leaves and I lock the door behind him, Katee lets out a little squeal, and spins around the massive presidential suite.

"This place is gorgeous." She continues to spin, taking it all in. "I mean, the chalet was awesome too, but this place." She rushes to the window and opens the curtain. "Look at the view, Luke."

I step up behind her, press my chest to her back and look out at the snowy peaks glistening beneath the near full moon. "It's something."

"I knew we would win," she says and claps her hand. "Although I'm not sure how you knew I was an ass girl."

I laugh. "You're pretty transparent, Katee, and I have known you since you were five. A guy picks up on these things."

She plants one hand on her hips, and it's all I can do not to stare at her curvy body. "Well, I know you're a leg guy."

"Oh, yeah?" I say. "How exactly do you know that?"

"A girl in a short dress and nice pair of heels, and you're a goner, Luke." She turns to me, and pokes my chest but I don't budge.

I step into her, press my legs to hers. "Maybe it's only your legs I like."

"And maybe it's only your ass I like."

"Is it?" I ask blatantly.

"Wouldn't you like to know." She squirms out from my hold and her eyes go to the rose pedals sprinkled across the bed. "They went all out for us."

I'm about to tell her I would like to know, when she folds her arms and hugs herself. Something inside me softens. "Hey, still cold. Fuck, we never should have come here."

"The dampness gets right into the bones, doesn't it?"

"Maybe alcohol will help warm you up." I pull the bottle of champagne from the ice bath it's in, and start untwist the wire cage.

"Alcohol makes me do lots of things," she teases.

"Oh, I know. But don't worry, I won't let you do anything you don't want to do." I pull the cork, and champagne spills over the edge.

"Ohmigod," Katee laughs and grabs us two glasses. I fill them, hand her one, and hold mine up in the air for a toast.

"What are we toasting to know."

"Tonight I'm going to get you warm." I say and step in to her, letting her know exactly where my thoughts are. "One way or another."

The air around us charges, sparks with the new, volatile electricity. I swallow against the suffocating sexual tension as my cock thickens, presses against my unforgiving zipper. I grip my glass tighter as my hands itch to strip her bare and touch her all over. How would she react if I tore her clothes from her body, ravished the hell out of her? I assume one of two things could happen: I'll either lose a nut, or we're going to have the best fucking night of our lives.

Time to find out.

"What...what did you have in mind?"

I tip my champagne glass and point to the big Jacuzzi tub in the corner of the room, a skylight on the ceiling over it. "For starters, I'm going to draw you a bath."

I cross the room, and following a path of rose petals and bend to fill the tub. I don't bother removing the petals from the bottom. Roses are her favorite, and they'll give off a nice fragrance for her bath. I test the water with my hand, and crook my finger.

She comes toward me, and her breathing is a little deeper than it was moments ago. I sit myself on the edge of the tub, and pull her to me, until she's standing between my legs. My hands go to the hem of her sweater.

"What are you doing?"

"Undressing you," I say, as I pull the sweater up and over her head, working hard to keep my cool when all I want to do is tear her clothes off, and have my way with her. Give her everything she's been missing and then some.

"I'm quite capable of undressing myself, Luke," she says, but her protest is weak, so fucking weak my pulse jumps in my throat. I swallow and work to keep my cool.

"I know." I toss her sweater to the floor, and my gaze goes to her lacy bra. I've seen her in it numerous times. Fuck, when she lived with me, all she ever walked around in was her bra and underwear, completely oblivious as to what that did to me. But tonight, oh, tonight she seems just a little more self-aware...and maybe a bit self-conscious.

She crosses her arms over her chest. "What are you doing?" I ask.

"I...uh..." she stumbles.

"I've seen you naked, Katee. You don't have to hide your-self from me."

I take her arms and put them at her sides. As I do, I lean

into her, and let my hot breath fall over her flesh. Little bumps break out on her skin and she visibly quivers.

Next, I go to work on the button on her jeans, and by this time, she's a little less stable on her legs. "Put your hands on my shoulders," I say. Her cool fingers grip my shoulders, and my dick thickens in response. Fuck, I'm in bad shape here. I pop the button, and the hiss of her zipper cuts through the quiet.

"I can do that," she says, but makes no attempt to help me. In fact, her nails are dragging skin as she holds on to me.

"It was just two days ago you asked me to help you take your pants off. You didn't seem to have a problem with me undressing you then."

"That's because they were all wet and I couldn't get out of them."

I shrug. "Doesn't matter. It's not like I haven't undressed you a time or two before, right?"

"I suppose," she says, her voice low and aroused. I look her over, read her body language, the way her eyes are glazed with desire, her lids fluttering like mad. Fuck man, she wants this—wants me. I resist the urge to take the gondola to the top of the mountain and scream hallelujah.

I help her from her pants, and take a moment to gaze at her near nakedness, and just like that my brain shuts down, unable to think of anything but the woman before me. With full breasts, curvy hips, long sexy, streamlined legs, her body is fucking beautiful.

"You're so damn perfect," I murmur.

She swallows and glances past my shoulders. "The tub is full," she says, and I reach down and turn off the faucet. She breathes deep. "The rose petals are so aromatic. My skin is going to smell amazing after bathing in them."

I can't wait to breathe her in, but I'm far more eager for a taste. My mouth waters, eager to get between her legs once and for all.

She looks over her shoulder, takes in the huge suite. "Um, what are you going to do while I bathe?"

I grin at her. "I'm going to wait for your answer."

"My answer?" she says, a stalling tactic because she knows damn well what I'm asking.

I tug my shirt off. "Actually, I think I'll get in with you." I tap the edge of the tub. "It is made for two, and I know how you are about water wastage."

Her gaze drops to my chest. "You really want to get in with me?" she asks her voice a low, barely-there whisper.

"Sure, why not?"

"Because..." She pulls her bottom lip between her teeth, like she can't bring herself to say what she really wants.

I put my hand on her thigh, run my thumb along her soft flesh. "Tell me what you want, Katee," I say, and her eyes fly to mine. A long pause and then, "If you can't tell me, show me." Her pupils expand, bleed into the brown as her pulse beats at the base of her neck. "I..." she begins but then stops and puts her hand on my body. I moan as she splays her fingers, touches me all over, but that moan turns into a growl of need when she slides her finger over my nipple, giving it a little squeeze. My heart jumps into my throat at her nonverbal response. She wants lessons between the sheets. Hot fucking damn!

I take her hand, bring it to my mouth for a kiss. "You catch on quickly," I say. "By the end of this week, the men in your bed are going to rock your world. Guaran—fucking—teed." Except, I hope, if I play this game right, she'll realize the only man she wants in her bed is me.

I reach around her, and in one smooth motion, unhook her bra. A little gasp catches in her throat. "That was pretty easy for you," she says as she folds one hand across her breasts, holding her bra to her body.

"Like I said, I'm good with my hands."

"And your stick," she says, then covers her mouth and laughs.

I laugh with her, but it comes out husky and needy. I angle my head, my thoughts going in a different direction. "You want to see the way I handle my stick, Katee?" I ask. Our eyes lock, hold, and when she doesn't answer, I tear open my pants. Her head dips and her mouth parts slightly. "Well, do you?"

"I...yes," she whispers.

"I like when you're honest like that."

"I'm always honest, that's what you love about me."

I grin. "I'll show you the way I handle my stick, but remember, it's tit for tat. You watch the way I touch myself and later, I get to watch you." Her eyes go impossibly wide as I kick my pants off and take my throbbing dick into my hand. A little whimpering sound catches in her throat as I fist myself and rub from base to tip.

"You like that, huh," I say, a statement not a question as she continues to make sexy sounds and shift her weight from one foot to the next. "You don't have to answer, Katee. Everything in the way you're acting tells me you like watching me fuck my hand." Pre-cum drips from my crown and I dip into it, use it for lubricant. "When I touch your body, those are the noises I want you to make. Talk dirty if you want. I'm your best friend, and this is about making sure you get what you need."

"Okay," she whispers, her lids fluttering as fast as the pulse at the base of her neck.

"Now drop your arms. I want to see all of you." She does as I say, and her bra falls to the floor.

"Motherfucker," I say and scrub my chin as I take in her

perfect breasts, her nipples all puckered and ready for my mouth. I wet my bottom lip, prepare it.

"Like what you see?" she asks, turning my words back on me and I fucking love the playful side of her.

I slowly lift my gaze to hers, not wanting to tear my eyes from her body. "Yeah, I do."

A little bolder than she was moments ago, she grips her panties, and tugs them down her legs. She stands back up, giving me a perfect view of her bare body.

"You're perfect," I say.

"No, I'm not—"

"Hey," I say, and shake my head no to stop her. "You're perfect. Got it."

"You are too. I want..." She lets her words fall off, but I'll have none of that. Tonight is all about her, pushing her to ask for what she wants, one way or another.

"What do you want, Katee?"

She swings her arm out, and then brings it back to her side. "Can I touch you?"

"You've touched me a million times." I take my hand from my cock. "You never asked before. Why now?"

"Because I've never touched you here." She closes her fingers around my dick, and my hips automatically jerk forward.

"Fuck, Katee. That feels good."

"So you think you can make me come, Luke?"

My dick jumps at her boldness, the blatant way she put that out there. "I know I can."

Her lids lift. "Pretty confident. I like that."

"I'm going to show you exactly what sex should be like for you. I'm going to fucking worship every inch of you, and make you come so goddamn hard, you might just lose your mind." Heat dances in her eyes, as her grip on my dick tightens. "I'm going to make you moan, Katee. Better yet, I'm going to make you scream, and you're going to talk so fucking dirty we might just have to wash your mouth out with soap."

"Here I'd rather have something else in my mouth," she says and I can't help but laugh as she totally gets into this, ready to have some fun. With her hand still on my cock, she lifts one leg and puts it into the tub. "Mmm, it feels amazing."

"My cock or the water?" I ask.

She chuckles. "Both."

Even though I'm ready to follow through with my promises, I need to warm her body, plus a little extra foreplay never hurt anyone. I hold her as she lifts her other leg and climbs in. Her hand falls from my dick, as she submerges to her shoulders. "Plenty of room for two," she says.

I slide in behind her and she leans against me. I adjust her a bit, so she's not crushing my nuts. Her head lifts and she gazes at the stars through the skylight. "A girl could get used to this," she says as I reach around her, take her breasts into my hands. I rub my thumbs over her nipples and she presses into me. I pinch slightly, and she gasps. I let go, and lightly stroke her pebbled nubs to ease the sting.

"Katee, there are so many things I'm going to do to you."

"Like what?" she asks, her voice shaky as I slide my hand lower, until it's between her legs.

"First I want to show you there is nothing wrong with you by giving you a mind-blowing orgasm," I say, and she takes a fast breath.

"What if I can't?"

I hear real worry in her voice. "You can. I'm going to learn your body, and give you everything you need. I promise you that, and you know I'm a man of my word." That gives me pause. Am I betraying her trust by not telling her what I'm really up to? I'm not sure, but I can't take a chance on losing her if she doesn't feel the same.

"I love that about you," she whispers.

"Oh, is that what you love about me?" I tease.

I lightly stroke her folds, then pull them apart. When I touch her clit, her hips lift and she lets loose the sexiest bedroom noise. Nice. "I'm going to spend a lot of time right here," I say, as her clit swells beneath my touch.

"Yes," she whispers. I play with her pussy, and her legs fall open against the side of the tub. Jesus fuck, I can't wait to get my mouth on her, my cock inside her. But I've been wanting her like this for so many goddamn years, I'm sure I'm going to blow my load before we even get started—especially if she gives me one of her porn star blowjobs.

She grows silky wet beneath my touch and before the water washes away all her lubricant, I ask, "Are you warm now?"

"Yes," she murmurs. "I'm hot, actually."

I laugh at that. "Good, now let me get you on that bed and heat you up a whole lot more."

I stand, and help her from the tub. Water drips down her neck and pools on her nipple. I've never seen a sexier sight. She grabs two towels off the fancy gold towel tree and hands one to me.

She dries herself as she crosses the room, and I can't help but feel a measure of nervousness now that I've set this plan into motions. This is Katee, not some random bunny who sleeps around, and this is a delicate situation. I want to do right by her. Want to give her what she needs while proving how good we can be. I can only hope that by the end of the week, she sees me as more than a best friend.

Don't fuck this up, dude.

KATEE

I reach the bed and turn to see if Luke has followed me. He's slowly making his way toward me, the intensity of his gaze unlike anything I've ever seen before. It burns through me, takes the air from my lungs until I'm a little lightheaded, unsteady on my feet. I hold the towel to my needy body as my skin comes alive, everything in me wide awake and aware that my best friend is a *real* guy, and right now he has a major erection aimed my way.

I'm going to have sex with my best friend!

He stops walking and angles his head. His gorgeous blue eyes move over my face. "Second thoughts?" he asks, like he can read my mind, which he probably can. No one knows me quite the way he does.

I take one quick minute to think about it, then shake my head. "No. I want this." Not only do I want to know what I've been missing out on, I want Luke's hands on my body, his cock inside me. It's insane really, considering we've known each other forever, and have always stayed within the friend zone. But ever since we watched porn, and he put the idea of sex in my head, I can't get it out. I'm pretty sure, the only way to move past this, and save the friendship, is to climb between the sheets with him. It's the only way I can get sex with him out of my brain. I'm sure come tomorrow I'll be back to normal, with a better understanding of how a guy should rock my world between the sheets. I take a breath and let it out slowly. Okay, girl, you've got this. I'm about to lay on the bed when I notice Luke hasn't moved. "Wait, do you still want to do this?"

"Oh, yeah," he says, and the amount of relief I feel is a little bit crazy. His gaze rakes over me possessively as he kicks one leg out to set himself back into motion, stalking toward me like a man on a mission. When it comes right down to it, I guess he is. I take in his beautiful body, his impressive cock, and an unfamiliar, tingly heat races through my veins, settles deep between my quivering legs. If I don't soon sit, I'm going to fall.

"On the bed," he commands, in a tone I've never heard him use with me before. "Legs open, hands grabbing those slats." He gestures toward the headboard and my body vibrates. Sex has always been vanilla, but something tells me this man likes a little kink.

I let my towel slide down my body, and my heart crashes against my ribs as I settle myself on the bed, and spread my thighs for him. Without ever taking his eyes off my body, he walks around me, picks up his champagne glass and takes a sip. Desperate for him to touch me, do something, anything, I widen my legs more, and my pussy lips spread.

"Mmm," he says, his gaze latching on to my sex. "Such a pretty shade of pink."

"Luke," I growl.

"Yeah," he says lazily, but I can sense his urgency. He's trying to take this slow. While I appreciate that he's deliberately unhurried for my sake, there is a desperate sort of need taking up residence between my legs

"Please..."

"You want my cock, Katee?" He arches a brow, and the corner of his mouth turns up in a playful smile. My God, he's the hottest guy on the planet. I mean, I always thought he was good looking, but this feral energy he's exuding—this alpha side of him—it's messing with me in the strangest ways. It must be some kind of chemical imbalance from watching porn and thinking about sex for the last twenty-four hours. "You want me to fuck that sweet pussy you have on display for me?"

"Yesss," I hiss at his delicious dirty talk. "I want your cock in me. I want you to make me scream."

He falters for a brief second, and I kind of like that I can mess with this calm façade he's trying so hard to present. He pulls himself up to his full height, and I'm impressed at how fast he gathers himself, and starts moving around me again. Warm fingers touch my thigh, a soft caress as he slides his big hand between my legs.

"I might want to fuck you with my fingers and mouth first," he says. "I want you wet and hot and begging for my cock." He lightly strokes my sex, prolonging the foreplay, and I cry out as my clit throbs. "Are you hurting for it, Katee?" he asks as he inserts a finger, and just holds it there, unmoving.

"Yes." I move my hips, shake my body, anything to get him to move his finger already.

"You still think I can't make you come?"

"No. I'm already close."

His chuckle vibrates through me, but he's not as in control as he'd like me to believe. There's a needy tremor in his tone, a slight shake to his hands as he touches me.

"So nice and wet," he says, and I lift my hips when he pulls his finger out. He brings it to his mouth, and sucks on it.

"Motherfucker," he murmurers. "I've never tasted anything sweeter."

I grip the slats tighter. "When do I get to taste?" I ask, just to provoke a reaction from him.

He falters slightly again, and I keep the smile from my face. "Don't worry. I'll give you a taste later. Right now, all this sweet juice is just for me. I'm not into sharing just yet."

"Such a greedy guy."

"Oh, you have no idea," he says, and slides his finger back into me, instantly finding the magical bundle of nerves that has always mysteriously eluded every other guy.

"I can be greedy too," I say and move my hips as he fucks me with his finger.

He cocks a brow. "I've never know you to be greedy, Katee."

I glance at his cock. "After I give you a porn star blow job, I want all your cum."

"Fuck," he says on a shaky breath, and I bite my bottom lip, loving that I can rattle him like this, and surprised that I find it so easy to talk dirty to him. Never before have I been able to do that, not without fearing I'd sound silly, or that my partner would laugh at me. But Luke, he's not laughing. Oh no, he's not laughing at all. He grips his cock again, and as he strokes, little tremors tug at my sex. Jesus, he's seriously going to bring me to orgasm without even trying.

"Your turn, Katee Kat."

I chuckle at the nickname. He hasn't called me that in years. I slide one hand down my body, feeling the dampness in my trimmed pubic hair. Cripes, the only time I ever get this wet is when I'm alone and using lubricant.

"Show me what you like. Show me how you like to touch that hot little cunt of yours."

Oh, God!

I run my finger over my clit, slow at first, until it's all swollen and sensitive, then I dip a finger inside my sex, and press into my palm. I lift my hips, rotate them, and let loose a needy moan that seems to do something to Luke. As my muscles clench, I become fully aware that I'm masturbating in front of Luke. Heck, I've never touched myself in front of a guy before, and usually have sex with the lights off. By rights, I should be embarrassed, or at least self-conscious, but oddly enough I'm not. This isn't any old guy I'm with. This is Luke. A guy who has always been there for me, done everything for me. Why shouldn't he be the first to give me an orgasm? Show me what I've been missing out on in the bedroom.

"Stop," he commands in a low, tortured voice. His nostrils flare, but I don't take my hand away. No, I continue to play with myself and his breathing changes, becomes labored.

"What part of stop didn't you understand?" he asks through clenched teeth, and I have to say, I seriously love this side of him.

"It just feels so good."

"Not as good as I'm going to make you feel."

He climbs onto the bed and falls over me, taking my hand from between my legs and replacing it with his own. "This," he says, giving my sex a squeeze. "This is all mine now. Got it?"

"Got it," I say, my entire body on hyperdrive, so damn anxious for him to do all the dirty thing things he's promised. Who knew I'd like a filthy-talking hockey player, or that I'd want to talk dirty right back to him? Here I was always a little self-conscious about myself in bed. Body image issues left over from my youth. But with him, I'm anything but. Probably because he's the guy who always made me feel better about myself, despite my size, and my dyslexia. The question is, will I be so free with the next guy I date? Or am I only able to let go with my best friend?

"You're going to want to hold on," he says pulling my thoughts back as he gestures to the slats. "This might get a little rough." His mouth closes over mine, and I taste the champagne on his tongue as I grip the headboard. I move beneath him, writhe like a needy woman, letting him know exactly how he's making me feel.

"That's it, Katee Kat, moan for me, show me how much you like it."

He angles his head, pressing his lips harder against mine. My God, the man is a good kisser. I grip the slats as he devours me, his tongue sliding over my lips and tasting my mouth with heated eagerness.

"This mouth," he says, putting his finger inside it. "I can't wait to feel it wrapped around my cock." I make a move to sit up, give him what he wants, but he stops me. "No, no, Katee Kat. It's not like that," he murmurs his breath hot on my skin. "It should never be like that."

"Like what?" I ask.

"It's ladies first, sweetheart. I don't ever want you with an asshole who doesn't understand that, okay?"

I swallow. Hard. "I've never been with a guy like that."

"That's because you've never been with the *right* guy."

Is Luke the right guy?

Oh, shit what am I saying. Of course he's the right guy. He's just not my guy.

He mouth closes over mine again, and his lips linger for a second. The next thing I know he's pressing open mouth kisses to my neck, and my pulse jumps beneath his lips.

"I want to touch you," I murmur.

"Soon," he says. "Soon you're going to be on your knees, and I'm going to feed you my cock, but right now, it's my turn. I want to touch and kiss every damn inch of you."

Soft mewling sounds escape my throat, because yeah, I want that too. He goes lower, and his hard cock presses against my leg. His hot mouth closes around one nipple as his hand goes to the other. "These nipples," he whispers against my skin. He pinches one and I yelp. "Look how needy they are for my mouth." I lift my head as he brushes the soft blade of his tongue over my turgid nipple, and it swells even more beneath his ministrations. "Perfect size, perfect taste," he says and drags one between his teeth. He rolls it around, until pleasure and pain merge, but goddammit, I like it. I like it a lot. Luke needs to know that. I need to tell him.

"Harder," I say, and he pauses for a second. "Luke, please." He clamps down again, and I cry out, pleasure zinging through my body. He licks my nub, a soft caress, and then his mouth goes to my other breast, giving it the same treatment. Honest to God, who knew I'd like a little pain in the bedroom?

He moves down my body, until his mouth is inches from my quivering sex. He kisses my stomach, lingers on my belly button. By now I'm panting, my mouth so damn dry it's hard to swallow.

"You okay?" he asks, when I choke a bit.

"Throat is dry," I murmur. "I'm going to need your cum."

"Jesus, fuck, Katee. You say shit like that to me and I'm going to come before I ever get inside you."

He grabs the champagne glass, and I lift my head as he gives me a small drink. Instead of placing it back on the nightstand, he dips his finger in and rolls it over my nipples. The tiny bubbles burst on my body, and I nearly freaking orgasm when he bends and licks me clean. He pours a bit of the bubbly on my stomach and it pools in my belly button.

"Body shots," he murmurs and drinks from my body. He dips his finger in again, and brushes the champagne over my clit, and I nearly levitate off the bed.

"Yes..." I cry out.

"So fucking responsive," he says and finishes the champagne in the glass. He sets it aside, roughly grips my thighs and spreads me more. "This hot little cunt," he says, and strokes my clit. "So wet and tight, I'm afraid once I get my cock in here, I might just destroy you."

I whimper. "I'm a big girl. I can handle it."

At least I think I can. I've never been with a guy his size before, a guy who looks like he's going to eat me alive. Dammit, I can't wait.

"Yeah, but I'm going to fill you with all my cum, and the porn star blow job will have to wait."

I groan but it turns into a moan when he licks me from bottom to top. "You want my cum in here?" he asks, and inserts a thick finger. I toss my head to the side, and moan. "I'll take that as a yes."

His mouth closes over my sex, and he eats me, devours me, his finger working miracles inside me. I move my hips, show him what he's doing to me. "You like me fucking you with my finger?"

"Luke..."

"Take one hand off the slats, and show me." I remove one hand and press it to his head, guiding his mouth back to my clit. He chuckles, his hot breath centered on my clit. I buck against his mouth, grind shamelessly. Pleasure races through me, centers between my legs. He slides another thick finger into me, and I cry out, as every nerve fires. He finds a rhythm with his fingers, and his lazy licks become firmer, the pressure on my clit taking me to the precipice.

"Luke," I cry out. "I'm...ohmigod, Luke..." My body explodes from pleasure, soaking his hand and mouth. He stays between my legs, lapping up all my juices, drinking me in and moaning like I'm the best thing he's ever tasted.

My body vibrates, clenches, and I think I might have torn a few muscles, but oh my God, it was worth it. Never have I come so hard before, with such intensity.

He goes back on his heels, and wipes the moisture form his face. There is a small, satisfied grin on his mouth. "That, my little Katee Kat, is how it's supposed to be done. Every fucking time."

"Jesus, I've been missing out."

"So have I," he says so low that I'm not sure I heard him right. I'm about to ask until I see how swollen his cock is. Poor guy needs some attention, too. I sit up, take him into my hands, and stroke. His hips jerk, and I lean forward, take him into my mouth.

"Katee, fuck. We can't. I'll blow a load down your throat and I seriously need to put my cock in you."

"But I want to taste you," I say, even though I like the idea of his cock inside me.

"Tomorrow. Tomorrow, you can get down on your knees and suck me all day. Right now, I want your pussy back on display for me."

We're going to do this again tomorrow? I mull that over for a second, not sure it's a great idea. Not that I don't love what we're doing. I do. But damn, he might just ruin me for any other guy.

"Now, Katee. On the bed, and spread for me."

I fall back and open my legs. "Is this how you like to fuck, Luke?"

"For now, we're going to fuck this way." He pets my sex, soothing little strokes to prepare me for his girth. "But I'm going to take you in every fucking position. Under me, on top of me, on your knees, and even up against the wall."

"Oh," I say. "I've only done missionary."

"And that's why we're going to do it all. How else will you know what you like?"

"True."

He slides off the bed, and I instantly miss his heat. "What are you doing?"

"Condom," he says and fishes one from his bag. He comes

back to the bed, and settles on his knees between my spread legs.

I don't take my eyes off him as he tears into it and sheathes himself. Once done, he taps my ass. "Lift."

Not sure what he's up to I lift my hips and he slides a pillow underneath me.

"Oh," I say as he aligns my sex with his. "This isn't quite the missionary position."

"Missionary with a twist," he says, and grips my hips. He drags me to him, and grabs hold of his cock. I take a breath, eager for him to fill me. "This way I get to see your face when you come for me."

"I'm not sure I can come again," I admit honestly, and he angles his head.

"Yeah, you will." He positions his cock at my entrance, and holds my hips for leverage as he slowly slides in to me, offering me only one glorious inch at a time. My eyes roll back in my head as he stretches me.

"Doing okay, Katee?"

"That feels so damn good."

"Your sweet cunt is squeezing my cock so goddamn hard, this might be over before it begins." He enters me fully, seating himself high and excitement floods my system. I take in his face, the tortured way he's clenching down on his teeth. Once again my body begins to heat up, and my clit starts to throb all over again. I've never in my life had two orgasms in a row, but this man...well, I'm not sure what he's doing to me. I only know that I like it. As I think about that, my mind rewinds, thinks back to how I thought it would be weird if Luke stopped treating me like one of the guys. Well, um, okay, maybe it's not so weird, and maybe being treated like one of the girls is so much better.

I move my hips, encouraging him to fuck me. He starts moving, slow at first, but as his cock warms my body and creates friction against my G-spot, I begin shaking, and panting. Jesus, the man fucks like a God.

"That's so goooooddd," I cry out, and grab the slats to hold on. "Harder," I cry out. "Fuck me hard, Luke."

"Jesus," he murmurs, and picks up the pace. He slams into me, blunt, fast strokes that rattle my brain. His fingers bite into my hips, and will undoubtedly leave a bruise come tomorrow. He groans and grunts, and I love all the sex sounds he makes. Our eyes meet, lock, and we're both breathing so hard, I'm sure we're going to deplete the room of oxygen.

"I've never been fucked like this before," I manage to get out.

He pulls almost all the way out, then drives back in again. I move against the pillow, my breasts bouncing. "That's a goddamn shame," he says and slides one hand up my body to cup my breasts. He rubs the rough pad of his thumb over my nipple, and frissons of electricity travel straight to my core.

I revel in his touch, the way he fucks, until nothing exists but this moment and this man. I cry out his name, and in return he calls mine and I'm a little surprised how much I like hearing it on his tongue as he pounds into me. He stretches my sex, and I squeeze around him. My body so close to another release. His other hand leaves my hip and he presses his finger to my clit. Sparks zap my sex, and I want to hold on longer, want to fuck him like this until tomorrow morning, but the triple assault takes me over the edge, and I let go, coming all over his beautiful cock. As intense pleasure overcomes me, I pinch my eyes shut to ride out the delicious waves.

"I feel you," he says, and I open my eyes to see his hips curl forward as he put every inch of himself inside me. It's the most beautiful sight I've ever seen.

"Luke, I say, and reach for his arm, close my hand around it. His muscles bunch beneath my touch, and I squeeze around his cock. He pulls almost all the way out, slams back in again and tosses his head back.

"Motherfucker," he groans as he releases high inside me. I moan as each hard pulse expands my walls, and I wrap my legs around him to keep him high inside me. He holds my hips again, his touch softer, far more gentle than earlier. His eyes open, zero in on me. For a brief second, I wonder if there is going to be any awkwardness between us, but then his mouth curls up, and I smile at him.

"So that's how I should be fucked, huh?"

"Every single time." He puts one hand on my sex, lightly circles my sensitive clit. "You deserve to be worshipped."

He quickly removes the pillow and falls over me, crushing me beneath his weight. "Tomorrow I might bend you over that coffee table," he says against my ear as he peppers my face with kisses.

"Would this be before or after the porn star blowjob?"

He laughs, rolls over and discards the condom. A moment later he's beside me again, and pulls me on top of him. I rest my head on his chest and listen to his strong heartbeat. Without conscious thought, I circle his nipple with my finger.

His breathing changes, levels off, and I lift my head to see him. He opens one eyes.

"Katee."

"Yeah."

He opens his mouth like he wants to say something, then frowns.

"What?" I ask.

"Sleep," he says.

I lay back on him, and my body is still so high, I'm not sure I can sleep. Sex with him was amazing. Goddammit, a girl could get used to this. Too bad he's just helping me out in the bedroom while we're on a fake honeymoon.

Too bad?

Wait, what am I thinking? This is my best friend. No way, no how can I start falling for him, especially when he has a woman waiting for him at home. She might have broken his heart, but she's the one he loves, right? I'm the one he's just doing a favor for.

Oh, man, I never should have had sex with him. It's already starting to mess up my brain. If only it hadn't been so good. Good? More like mind-blowing amazing. Okay, tomorrow morning when he wakes up, I'll tell him this was a bad idea. That I already learned a lot, and we shouldn't spend any more time between the sheets. Yeah, I'll tell him all those things.

Or not.

9

LUKE

I wake up and turn my head to find Katee sleeping soundly beside me. My mind races back to last night, and holy hell, what a fucking night it was. I'm surprised I lasted as long as I did, considering she's been the star of my bedroom fantasies for a hell of a lot of years.

With the sheets kicked to the foot of the bed, I reach down and cover her naked body, but not before gifting myself with a good long look. My God, she's the most beautiful woman in the world. And I just had sex with her.

I'm not sure how she'll feel about it this morning, but last night she was totally into it—into me. It's hard to believe no guy has ever satisfied her. Jesus, she came to life under my touch and had no trouble showing me what she liked. I grin at that. I kind of like that I'm the only guy who's ever done that for her. I quietly climb from the bed, leaving her to sleep as I go in search of coffee. All the supplies I had stocked at the chalet had been moved here. I find the grounds, and fill the coffee maker. As it brews, I make a quick trip to the bathroom. By the time I finish, I step back into the massive presidential suite, and Katee is nowhere to be found.

What the fuck?

I feel a measure of panic. Jesus, have I scared her off? Was having sex with my best friend the worst decision of my life? I grab a fistful of hair and tug, and that's when I feel a cold breeze wash over me. I turn and find Katee outside in nothing but a big white robe. I grab mine from the closet, shove on the slippers provided, and step outside with her.

"You're going to freeze to death out here," I say. She's about to turn around but I step up behind her, and pull her against my chest. I slide my arms around her body, and hug her to me.

"It's so beautiful out here. I bet the sunrise is gorgeous."

"Maybe tomorrow we can set the alarm."

She nods, and her hair tickles my nose. I stare off in the distance, take in the gorgeous town with all the mountains and valleys. "I guess this wasn't such a bad honeymoon location after all."

She chuckles. "It's not the beach, but we can still go swimming. This hotel has a pool."

"I didn't pack a suit," I say.

"I'm sure there's a gift shop where we can get you one."

"Please don't make me go shopping." My stomach takes that moment to grumble and Katee laughs. "I guess I worked up quite an appetite last night," I say, using my hunger to open up the conversation about what happened last night.

"Me too."

"Katee." She turns in my arms and when she smiles up at me, I let loose a breath. "How are you feeling today?"

She absently twirls her hair around one finger, and looks down for a moment. "I've used muscles that I haven't used in years."

"Skiing will do that to you," I tease.

She pinches my nipple through my robe, then her eyes go wide. "Oops."

"Oops, my ass," I say, and she chuckles. "We're good, right?" I ask.

"We're good, Luke. We're better than good." She rests her head on my chest, and my heart pounds a little harder.

"So then you're going to let me bend you over the coffee table, show you how good sex can be in different positions?" She nods, but it feels tight against my body. "What?"

She lifts her head and smiles but I know her well enough to know it's forced. "I need food," she says.

I want to press, but maybe she just needs time to process. "Why don't you get a shower, and I'll have your coffee ready for you when you're done."

"Sounds good."

"Where do you want to go to breakfast?" I ask

She rubs her stomach. "All I want is a protein shake."

"Like hell. We're on our honeymoon, and we're indulging."

"Luke..." She sticks her stomach out. "I'm going to have a big muffin top when I leave here if I'm not careful."

"Haven't I told you how much I like muffins." I lick my lips, and lust moves into her eyes. She reaches for my nipple again but catches herself.

"Go ahead," I say. "I dare you."

She squeals and dashes off to the bathroom, closing the door behind her. I go back to the kitchen and take two mugs from the cupboard. I toss in a splash of milk, and catch sight of the package Veronica gave us for winning the game. "Hey, should we go on the helicopter ride today?" I dig through the brochures and read about the tour until the coffee maker beeps. I fill our cups and walk to the bathroom. I call out to Katee, but she can't hear me with the water running.

I take a sip of my coffee and my damn cock thickens as I picture her in there soaping up her gorgeous body. Goddammit, I need her again. Fuck, last night was just a teaser, a taste of how good things are between us and I want more. Honest to fuck, no matter how many times I take her, it will never be enough to sate my need.

I open the door, and from behind the glass door, Katee is running her hands all over her body.

"Hey," I say, and she yelps.

"You scared me." She wipes steam from the glass. "What are you doing?"

I set her coffee down. "Bringing you coffee."

"Oh, thanks." I stand there a moment longer, and she says, "Ah, and what are you doing now?"

I lean against the counter, and cross my ankles. "Now I'm watching you wash."

"It's a little intrusive, don't you think?"

"I was inside you last night, Katee. Are you forgetting that?"

A needy moan reaches my ear. "No, I could never forget that," she says.

"I was thinking."

"About?"

I slip out of my robe. "That this is a good opportunity to show you how awesome shower sex can be."

The glass door slides open and her gaze drops to my swollen cock. "I always thought shower sex was hard."

I grip my cock and stroked it. "Oh, it's hard, all right."

Katee backs up as I step into the large tiled shower, two rain shower nozzles hanging from the ceiling at either end, as well as nozzles on the wall. I look at all the faucets. Christ, a guy needs an engineering degree to figure out how to work all the taps.

"Nice shower," I say, and slide my hand around her waist and drag her soapy body to me. I run my hands down her back, and grab her ass cheeks. I squeeze a little.

"My, you have grabby hands this morning," she teases.

"The better to touch you with."

"As long as I get to touch, too." She reaches for the soap and puts it on my chest, and I let loose a groan as she washes me. Her soft hands slide over my chest, and then she turns me around to do my back. "It's going to take a lot of scrubbing, Katee. I'm pretty dirty."

"The only dirty thing on you is your mouth. That's what needs to be washed out with soap," she says and chuckles. I laugh with her, but it turns to a moan when she reaches around my body and captures my throbbing dick. She slides her hands over it, the soap making my cock slippery.

"The feels so fucking good."

She lets go, and steps around me. I put my hands on her body, but she backs me up until I'm under the spray. The water rinses my body clean, and she turns off the faucet. "What are you doing?" I ask.

She has a small smirk on her face as she drops to her knees before me, settling herself on the tile. She leans forward and licks my crown and I nearly lose my shit then and there.

"Mmm," she says, and cups my balls, giving them a little massage. "Shower sex *is* hard," she teases, and when she opens her mouth, offering it up to me, I grip the back of her head and feed her my cock. Her lips widen to accommodate my girth and the sight of her on her knees doing this for me rocks my fucking world. She takes me deep, and I hit the back of her throat. Her hands grab my ass, and she grips me, rocking into me and sucking me off like a pro.

"Jesus fuck, you're killing me, Katee," I growl.

She chuckles against my cock, and works both her hand and mouth over me. I hold the wall with one hand and the back of her head with the other as she kneels there and worships the shit out of my cock. I'm so hard, so close, I can't hang on for another second. She must sense it. She angles her head to see me, and I try to take my dick from her mouth when she sucks it in deeper.

"You want my cum?" I ask.

She makes a soft mewling sound around my cock, and when she takes me to the back of her throat, I let go. She gobbles me up, swallows every last fucking drop and it's the hottest goddamn thing I've ever seen. Not because she just gave me a porn star blow job, but because I'm in love with this woman, and she's doing this to please me. I finally stop spurting, and reach down and pull her to me.

"You're fucking amazing," I say, and wipe my fingers over her lips. I turn the spray back on to warm her body and place her under it. She has a glazed look in her eyes, a sweetly satisfied smile on her face. "You're damn good at that," I say.

"You liked it, huh?"

"Fuck yeah, I liked it."

"So you'll let me do it to you again?"

"Katee, anytime you want to suck my cock, just say the word."

She laughs hard at that, but it turns into a yelp when I spin her around. "But now I get to do things to you."

"Ooh," she says, her voice full of arousal. "What kind of things?"

"Dirty things, Katee." I say and place her hands on the wall. From the overhead spray, water drips down my back as I step into her. "Don't move them," I warn.

I take in her beautiful body, her sweet ass and long sexy legs. "These legs," I say, and run my hands over her outer thighs. "I want them wrapped around my neck tonight." She visibly quivers, and I slide my hands up to her neck. I push her wet hair away and kiss her neck. She quakes beneath my touch. I grab the nozzle from the wall, remove it from the hook and adjust the spray.

"Open your legs," I say.

She inches her legs apart, and I reach around her, center the spray right on her clit.

"Ohmigod," she cries out.

"What, you've never done this before?" I ask.

"Well, maybe a time or two," she says and chuckles.

"Did you make yourself come like this?"

She nods, and I love how open she is with me. I move the spray around and her hips rotate. "Feel good?"

"Yes," she whimpers.

I center the spray back on her clit, and run my hand along the crevice of her ass. She stiffens beneath me, and my heart races. Little Katee hasn't been touched here before. "Bend forward a little for me," I say, and she does, tipping her sweet ass in the air. "You are so fucking sexy."

I slide a finger into her tight pussy, and she's so goddamn lubricated I nearly lose my mind. "You're all wet, Katee. Did sucking my cock make you like this?"

"Yes," she says. "I liked being down on my knees for you. I like making you come, Luke. I know this is about helping me, but I want you to feel good, too."

"Always so concerned about me," I say.

"That's what you love about me."

"You think that's what I love about you?" I answer, and pull my finger from her hot cunt. She whimpers at the loss but then goes stiff when I run my finger around her puckered passage.

"Luke," she says her voice uncertain.

"Yeah, Katee Kat?"

"I've never..."

"I know."

"I'm not sure I'll like it."

"How will you know if you don't try?"

As I tease her back passage, just putting the tip of my pinkie inside her, I hold the spray closer to her clit, increasing the pressure, and she whimpers. "Why don't you hold this nozzle for me," I say. She takes the nozzle, and holds it to herself, and I push a finger inside her tight pussy. I play with her, run my finger along her G-spot, and lightly toy with her ass. Her hips begin moving, swaying and little cries catch in her throat. "That's it, Katee. Come all over my fingers."

She bucks against my fingers, and holds the wall with one hand as she manipulates her clit with the nozzle.

"Luke," she cries out. "I'm…"

Her words fall off as she tumbles into an orgasm. Her hot juices soak my hand, and I fucking love seeing her like this. She's breathing hard, hell so am I, and my goddamn cock is hard again, desperate to get back inside her. I remove my finger from her ass, and take the nozzle from her. I hang it back on the hook and spin her to face me. Her eyes are heavy lidded; her lips are parted. I step into her and her eyes widen when she feels how hard I am.

"Can you take me?" I ask.

"Yes," she whimpers.

I'm about to turn her again, when I remember I don't have a condom. "Shit."

"What?"

"I don't have protection."

"Do we need one?" she asks and nibbles her bottom lip.

"I always use a condom."

"I know, which means you're clean."

"Yeah, I am."

"I'm on the pill, and besides, it's me, Luke."

My heart squeezes, and I put my hand on her face, brush my thumb over her cheek. "Yeah, it's you. I wouldn't ride bareback with anyone but you."

That brings a smile to her face. "Same. Now can you please fuck me and fill me with your cum."

"I'm going to fill you with so much cum, it's going to drip out of you all day."

"Good," she whispers. "Every time I feel it, I'll brush my tongue over my bottom lip so you'll know."

"That will drive me fucking crazy," I say as I put my cock at her entrance.

"Yeah, I know." She chuckles and I grip her shoulders. In one quick thrust, I'm high inside her and she's gasping for breath.

"Luke, my God, that feels incredible."

I pump into her and she moves with me, our body in synch, like we've been doing this for a lifetime. We haven't been, we just should have been. Her body squeezes my cock, and she straightens a little. I snake one arm around her waist to hold her to me, the other hand goes to her breasts. I pinch her nipple.

"I believe I owed you that."

She moans her approval and I thrust into her, unable to get deep enough. Pleasure zaps my balls, and I press my lips to her back, kissing everywhere I can.

"Do you have any idea how good you fuck," she huffs out.

I laugh. "Never been this good for you before?"

"Hell no. I'm going to compare every guy to your high standards."

"Don't settle for anything less."

"I don't think anyone is going to live up to them."

Her words thrill me and I chuckle against her skin, as her sex clenches around my dick. She's so fucking close. "Then I guess you'll just have to keep fucking me," I say, and as soon as the words leave my mouth, she climaxes. "Look at you, coming all over me again."

"Luke," she cries out and closes her hands over mine, holding them tight against her body.

"Katee, I'm going to fill you with my cum now."

"Yes, please." I drive in deep, seat myself high, and let go.

"Fuck me," I cry out.

"I feel you. Your cum is so hot." I come and come and come, and when I'm finally depleted, I drop my head to her shoulder, unable to get my breath.

"So good," she cries out. We stay in that position for a long time. My cock inside her, one hand on her stomach, the other on her breasts. Our breathing finally regulates but I have no desire to move. I could stay right where I am forever, but I'm pretty sure she needs to rinse off, sit down, and get some coffee into her.

I back her up, and the warm spray falls over us.

"I think shower sex is my favorite," she whispers and we both laugh.

"Not so fast," I say. "We have a lot more positions to try out."

"I don't think I'll make it."

She's not the only one. Come the end of the week, if things don't work out between us, I'll be the one in real fucking trouble of not making it.

10

KATEE

"**O**hmigod, this view is amazing," I say to Luke as I glance out the window of the helicopter. We were lucky that they had a cancellation and we were able to book it fast. The pilot takes us over a huge mountain and when we reach the other side, numerous skiers are weaving their way down a sugary hill. I wave to them, but I don't think any of them can see me.

Luke is grinning at me when I turn his way. "You love this."

"I do. I've never been in a helicopter before." I grab my phone from my pocket and start taking pictures. "Where's your phone?" I ask. "You might want to get a few pictures."

He shrugs. "It's back at the suite. I don't want to take any calls this week. I'm sure my inbox is full."

"What if Arianna is trying to call you?" I ask. "You might want to talk to her."

He scrubs his chin and turns from me. I put my hand on his leg and give it a squeeze, letting him know I understand he doesn't want to talk about it, but that I'm here for him just the same. Wanting to lighten his mood, I point to something near the tree line.

"I think there's a bear down there?"

"What, really?" He leans into me, and I breathe in his familiar scent as he looks out the window. "I think it's a wolf," he says.

The pilot glances down, and heads toward the tree line. "It's a wolf," he says. "I'll try to get closer so you can get a picture." I squeal with excitement, and Luke laughs at me. I'm thrilled to see his mood has shifted again, and he's enjoying this trip. The pilot heads close to the tree, but the sound of the engine scare the animal and it darts into the trees. I take some shots anyway. When I finish, Luke takes my hand and brings it to his lips. He kisses my fingers and says, "I'm glad you're enjoying this?"

"Are you?"

"Yeah. I'm glad you're here with me," he says, and I lean in to him.

"I'm so glad we won the game. Still we would have had a good time just doing nothing together."

"We always do."

I've always been close to Luke, but after all the intimacies we've been sharing, I feel even closer to him. Impossible I know, but true nonetheless. We continued to hold each other, and enjoy the gorgeous views as the pilot finishes our tour, taking us back to the air strip near the resort. Luke gives him a big tip and we hop back into the rental car. Dusk is upon us as we reach our hotel, and Luke hands the car keys to the bell hop.

I hurry inside out of the cold, and Luke saunters in behind me, like he's in no hurry to do anything. I let my gaze fall over him, but that's when I realize I'm not the only one looking. From behind, two girls are whispering and gawking at Luke. He comes up to me, and the jealousy I feel is a bit disconcerting. We're friends with benefits, and I have no right to feel possessive of him.

"Aren't you Luke Erikson?" the girl with the long dark hair asks as she comes up to him, completely ignoring me. Her friend however, a bleached blonde, isn't ignoring me at all. Nope, she's looking me over, and trying to figure out if I'm a threat to her at all. She tears her gaze away and beams at Luke. Well then, I guess she doesn't think I'm a threat at all.

"They call you the Stick Handler," she says and chuckles. "I'd love to get an autograph, and maybe we can meet up later for a drink. I'd love to hear all about the ways you handle your stick."

I glance at Luke, who's taking it all in stride, even though deep down he's a private guy who hates all the attention. I was really hoping no one would recognize him here, and he could use the time to relax after the horrible ordeal back home.

"I want an autograph, too," the brunette says, and unzips her coat. She widens her shirt and sticks out her cleavage. "Right here," she says and chuckles.

"Ladies," Luke begins, and puts his arm around me. "This is Katee. My wife. Someday we'd like to have children and if I autographed you there," he makes a face as he points to her cleavage, "chances are she'll remove a few body parts that will prevent that from happening. But if you have a pen and paper, I'd be happy to give you an autograph."

Their smiles fall as they look at me. "Oh, I didn't realize you were married," the blonde says, disdain in her eyes as she gives me the once over again.

The brunette fishes a pen and notepad from her purse. "We'll be at the bar tonight. Why don't you both come, have a drink with us."

"Sorry, but we can't. We already have plans."

"Well, if anything changes..." the girl says refusing to let it go. Goddammit, I'm standing right here. I shift from one foot to the next and think about tripping one of them. Luke gives the autographs, makes a bit more small talk, and then puts his arm around my waist to lead me away. I shake my head.

"Yeah, I know," he says.

I angle my head to see him. "Why did you tell them I was your wife?"

He gives a casual shrug. "Well, you are."

"No, I'm not. But that comment about having children was pretty funny." He laughs. "Would you have signed her fake boob if I wasn't standing there?" I ask, then wish I hadn't. I sound like a jealous wife, and before Ari came along, those were the kind of girls Luke would have been found hanging out with. I wasn't jealous then. At least I didn't think I was. Oh, God, maybe I was. Maybe I just buried all the things I felt. Knew better than to crush on my best friend.

Then again, maybe all this sex is messing with my emotions. I should probably put a stop to it right away. Or tomorrow.

"No. My boob signing days are behind me." He grins at me and nudges me with his shoulder. "Besides why would I want to see her breasts when yours are so perfect."

As we head to the elevators, I whack him in the gut. "Whatever." He bends forward and makes a big deal from the hit and I just roll my eyes at him. "What are these plans we have for tonight?"

"I booked the rooftop restaurant. A romantic candlelight dinner for two, then if I play my cards right, I'm going to play with those perfect breasts of yours."

We stop at the elevator and he jabs the button. "I'm sure you'll play your cards right, Luke. But before you do." I go up on my toes and put my mouth to his ear. "I'd love to give you another blow job. The last one didn't last long."

"Jesus, Christ," he says and laughs.

"What?" I ask innocently, and flutter my lashes at him.

"First, don't say stuff like that to me when we're in a lobby full of people." He glances over his shoulder and puts his hands in front of his crotch. "Second, how the fuck did you expect me to last? Jesus, that mouth of yours."

I chuckle, loving that we can tease each other like this, and that he really likes my mouth on him. I kind of like my mouth on him, too.

The doors open and we step on, and move to the back as other come in behind us. I lean against Luke, and melt into his body when he put his hands on my hip. I like how we fit together, how he's just so damn easy to be with. But in less than a week, he'll likely be back with Arianna, carrying forward with their plans to marry. A lump fills my throat. I really don't like that girl. Then again, have I ever really liked any of the women he's gone out with? None of them were good enough for him, as far as I was always concerned. Luke never really liked the guys I've dated either. I guess that's just the way it is with best friends.

The elevator stops a few times, and we're alone when we finally reach the top floor. There is only one other floor, and that's the rooftop restaurant, all glass panels to look out over the mountains.

We step off the elevator, and Luke lets us into our room. I still can't get over the fact that we're staying is such a posh place. "What time is dinner?" I ask, but let loose a little gasp when Luke grabs me, holds me against the closed door and kisses me, hard. When we break apart, I'm breathless.

"What was that for?" I ask and put my hand on his chest.

"For teasing the hell out of me when I couldn't do anything about it."

I grin at him. "Well, now that I know what the punishment is for teasing..."

"Oh, you think that's only kind of punishment I give out?"

"It's not?"

"No, and if you do it again, you'll see what real punishment is like."

A jolt of heat goes through me. There is a filthy side to my best friend that I never knew about, but goddammit, I like it. "Well, then..."

"Careful, Katee Kat," he says playfully, but the heat in his eyes turns me on even more and makes me want to experience his brand of punishment firsthand.

I swallow. "What time is dinner?" I ask.

He checks his watch. "One hour. Enough time for us to shower and dress."

He shrugs out of his coat and helps me off with mine. "I only packed one black dress. You know the one that has the buttons along the back and comes to above my knee."

"I know the one. It's perfect."

"What about you. Did you bring anything dressy?"

"Suit. It's in the closet."

"Oh, which one?" I ask, and walk to the closet to open it. When I do, I see his phone on one of the shelves. The little red light is flashing, indicating he has messages. I take in his dark suit, then shut the door. "I love that one on you."

"You should. You picked it out." I turn around to see him, and laugh when I find him standing there stark naked.

"What are you doing?'

He grins at me. "Getting ready for the shower. Why are you still dressed?"

"You definitely don't waste any time." I give him a wink.

"If you're referring to the blow job again, I—"

"I'm not, I'm not," I say, laughing as I strip down. My god, I love the way he looks at my body, like my curves are sexy and my flaws are non-existent.

"Next time, your mouth is going to get sore from sucking."

"Oh, is that right?"

I follow him in to the bathroom. "Yeah, that's right."

"Too bad, then."

He turns on the shower, and tests the temperature. Once it's hot, he reaches for my hand and drags me in.

"Why too bad?" he asks.

"Because if you were going to be fast again, I would have given you another right now, but I guess that can't happen since we don't want to miss our reservation."

"You know you're going to pay for that, right?" he says and puts me under the spray. The water feels glorious on my chilled skin, but not as nice as his hands do as he washes me.

"What did I do?"

"I never knew you were such a fucking tease." He shakes his head.

"And I never knew you liked a little kink."

He swallows. Hard. "What am I going to do with you?"

"I don't know, but I can't wait to find out."

LUKE

We step off the elevator and I glance around the dimly lit roof top restaurant. Katee's eyes are big as she takes in the opulence, as well as the view outside the floor-to-ceiling glass wall.

"Nice, huh?" I say, and take her hand in mine.

"This place is amazing."

The hostess comes up to us and I give our names. She smiles and showcases perfect white teeth. "Ah, you two are the winning honeymoon couple. Congratulations. Please come this way." We follow her to a quiet table in the corner, overlooking the slopes. "Best seat in the house," she tells us.

"Thank you," Katee says.

"Your server will be by to take your order, and I'll send over a bottle of champagne."

She places our menus in front of us, and Katee giggles. "Champagne."

My mind goes back to when I poured it over her belly. But I can't think about that right now. This is not the place for a hard on. "Remember when we were kids and you drank too much champagne?" I ask.

She waves her hand at me. "I'm not sixteen anymore. I can handle my liquor now."

"You danced on my patio table, nearly fell and broke your damn neck."

"Good thing you were there to catch me."

I nod. "I'll always be there to catch you," I say, and she goes quiet when the champagne arrives. The server introduces himself and presents the bottle. He uncorks it, and pours a splash into my glass. I taste it and nod in approval. The server fills Katee's, the, adds more to my glass.

Once he leaves, I says, "I had to carry you home and put you to bed."

"Thank God Mom wasn't home. She would have killed me." She goes quiet for a moment, like she's remembering the event, then says, "Wait, didn't I wake up in my pajamas?"

"I undressed you."

"Why would you do that?" She angles her head and pinches her lips tight. "Did you at least close your eyes?"

I laugh. "You couldn't go to bed in your clothes. You got sick all over them, and no, I didn't close my eyes."

She groans. "Luke...I didn't want you to see me like that, I was..."

"Perfect." She rolls her eyes at me, and we clink glasses. "To perfection," I say.

I open my menu, and quickly shut it. "That was fast," she teases and I shake my head at her.

"I'm getting—"

"Let me guess," she says and looks over the menu. "Surf and turf."

"You got it." She closes her menu. "I'm going to have the same." I take another sip of champagne, and look her over as she glances out the window. "Some of those kids are so good on skiis."

"Do you really not want kids?" I ask her.

She screws up her nose. "I don't know. I guess maybe someday, but I don't want to be a single mom, and marriage is out of the question."

"If the right guy came along, would you rethink it?"

She laughs. "I don't think there are any right guys for me, Luke."

I lean toward her. "Okay, describe your perfect guy. What would he look like, what would he do?"

"Hmm." She takes a sip of champagne. "This is so good," she says and I reach for the bottle to refill her glass. "Okay, well, I guess he'd be tall. I like tall guys."

"I'm tall."

"I know that. Anyway, I'd want him to be athletic. I would like for my kids to be sporty, and they're definitely not going to get that trait from me." Another sip of champagne. "Sunbathing on a beach is about as athletic as it gets for me."

"You went skiing."

"I slid down the bunny hill. Big difference." We both laugh. "I like dark hair on guys too. I've never much been into blond."

"I like dark hair on girls, too," he says.

Her head jerks back. "Um, Ari is a blond. A bleached blonde, but a blonde nonetheless. Actually, Luke, most of the women you've been with have been blonde."

"Go figure. What else do you like in a guy?"

"He has to be honest."

I avert my gaze and look out over the mountain. I hate that I can't tell her what really went on between Ari and me, and that what I'm really doing here is less about giving her lessons and more about trying to get her to want all of me the way I want her. I just hope to fuck Ari has come to her senses. But what if she hasn't? What if she still wants to go through with the wedding? I'm not about to, not when I don't love her. Will she turn spiteful, revengeful, do or say something to impact my career? Worry knots my gut, and I suck in a quick breath.

"Luke?" she asks.

"Go on," I say, working to pull myself together. "Tell me more."

"Okay, well, I like blue eyes."

"I have blue eyes."

"Yeah, you have the nicest blue eyes I've ever seen. Mine are boring brown."

I scoff. "Far from boring. You have the darkest eyes I've ever seen, Katee, and they're so expressive."

"Ah, so that's why you always know what I'm thinking?"

"Clean shaven or beard?"

She toys with the stem of her flute. "I like clean shaven, but I also like that scruff thing you're sporting," she says.

"Do you like the burn marks it leaves on your body?"

Her hand quivers and she nearly drops her glass. "Jesus, Luke."

I laugh. "You didn't answer the question."

"Yeah, I like it."

"I like it too. I also like when you licked your lips today, to let me know you could feel me dripping out of you."

The server comes back, and Katee has a flush on her cheeks as I give our orders. When the waiter leaves, I guide the conversation back to where we were. "What kind of job would your perfect guy have?"

"You know, I don't care, as long as he's happy doing what he does. He doesn't have to make a lot of money. You know that's not important to me."

"I know."

"So he could be a sports guy, on the road a lot and that wouldn't bother you."

"I'm used to that with you. I miss you when you're gone, though."

I reach across the table and take her hand in mine. "You know you could always come with me. A guy needs his own personal masseuse when he's on the road."

"Yeah, but what about when the kids come?"

"That's true. You'd be busy taking care of them."

She rolls her eyes. "What am I even saying."

"You're saying that there could be a guy out there for you."

The server comes back with a bowl of warm bread to get us started. Katee reaches for a slice, butters it and slides it into her mouth.

"Mmm, so good." She swallows, washes it down with another drink, and sits back in her chair. "Remember that time we used the bread machine to make pizza dough," she begins, and just like that we lose ourselves in old stories. Our meals come, and we eat, laugh, and drink too much champagne. Katee is giggly by the time we're finished.

"I need to go for a walk," she says. "Work off the food and champagne."

"Good plan." We take the elevator to our floor, change into jeans and sweaters, and bundle up in our winter coats before we head to the lobby. When we reach the main doors, we run in to Becca and Trey.

"Hey you two, how's the presidential suite?" Becca asks.

Color fills Katee's cheeks, and I grin. She must be thinking about all the fun things we've been doing in that suite.

"It's amazing."

Trey gestures toward the doors. "We were just heading to the club for drinks and dancing. Come with us."

"Sounds like fun, what do you think, Katee?" I ask.

"Let's do it."

We head outside and the cold air blasts our faces. Our Canadian friends don't seem to be bothered by it. Katee and

Becca talk about today's helicopter flight, while Trey and I talk hockey. Katee is shivering by the time we reach the club. I find us a table, and help her from her coat. She snuggles in next to me.

"I can never get warm here," she says.

"Did you read about the heated outdoor pool?" Becca asks. "I haven't tried it yet, but it's on my list of things to do."

"Now it's on mine."

The server comes and we all order a drink. "I probably shouldn't have anything. We had champagne at dinner."

"I think you worked it off with all that shivering," I say, and look out over the dance floor.

"What part of Canada are you from?" Katee asks our new friends.

"Calgary. You should come visit."

"Next time I play there, maybe Katee will come and we'll get together."

Katee gives me an odd look, but I don't comment on it. She's probably thinking that will never happen, because once this trip is over, Ari and I will be getting back together. But that's not what I want. I can't help but wonder if on some level Katee knows that. She knows I'm a one-woman kind of guy, and wouldn't sleep with someone if I was committed. I'm not a cheater, that's for sure.

A slower song comes on and I reach for Katee's hand. "Let's dance."

"Great idea," Becca says, and jumps up and drags a grumbling Trey to the dance floor. We laugh and fall in beside them. I pull Katee close and put my hands on her hips. We sway together, and as she brushes up against me, I dip my head and close my lips over hers. I kiss her softly, a slow caress over her bottom lip with my tongue and she exhales a soft sigh.

"You having a good night?" I ask.

"The best."

My hands fall lower, until I'm cupping her ass, and she chuckles against me. "I always thought you were a leg man, now I'm beginning to wonder."

"Have you seen this ass?"

"Hard to miss," I say.

She laughs. "You are perfect."

"You know what, Luke," she says, her voice thoughtful. She goes quiet, looks around the room, and says, "This whole vacation has been perfect. There isn't anyone else I'd rather go on a honeymoon with."

My heart leaps. Earlier tonight, when she described her perfect guy, she had me down to a T. I can't help but think I've opened her eyes to how good we are together and she's beginning to see me as more.

"It's not over yet," I say.

She puts her hand on my neck, and my pulse jumps beneath her soft fingers. "No, it's not," she says and goes up on her toes. I kiss her again, revel in the sweet taste of her mouth. When she breaks the kiss, a fast song comes on, and I stay on the dance floor with her, knowing how much she loves to dance. We used to dance all the time, before I became involved with Ari.

She throws her hands up in the air, and shakes her hips.

"You know you dance like no one is watching."

"I know, and that's what you love about me."

"You think that's what it is I love about you?" I ask. Soon enough I'm going to tell her exactly what it is I love about her, and I pray to fuck she feels the same way about me.

She turns around and shakes that sweet ass at me, teasing my cock until it's hard in my pants. I grip her hips and put my mouth near her ear. "You're so going to get it, Katee Kat."

I'm a bit light-headed and giggly by the time we make it back to our suite. Luke keeps one hand on me, and swipes the keycard over the lock. The door opens and we step inside. Elated after having such a wonderful night, I throw my arms around his neck and go up on my tip-toes. He grins at me, and it's so adorable all I want to do is rip his clothes off him and do dirty things together.

"That was so much fun," I say. "We haven't danced like that in ages."

His hands slide around my waist to hold me to him, and I don't miss the growing bulge between his legs. It fires my body, and the needy juncture between my legs pulses.

"I think you've had too much wine," he says.

I throw my hands up. "What can I say, I'm a lightweight."

Before I even realize what's going on, Luke picks me up, carries me across the room and sets me on the bed.

The warmth in his eyes curls through me, wraps around my wobbly heart. "I think you need sleep," he says, and unzips my coat. He pushes it from my shoulders and I just sit there and stare at his gorgeous body as he removes his own outwear and kicks off his boots.

"No, what I need is you," I say, as he kneels before me and tugs off my boots. "In this bed with me." As I look into his eyes, I know I don't just crave him, I need him, on a level that is almost frightening.

His nostrils flare as he looks at me. "You sure about that? If you had too much to drink…"

"You are such a good guy, Luke." I reach out and put my hand on his face, feel the roughness of his scruff on my palm. I revel in it for a moment, remember what it feels like between my thighs. "You always have my best interests at heart. But I'm a big girl. I know what I'm doing." I lift my other hand and crook my finger. "And I believe you said something like *you're going to get it*. What exactly am I going to get?" I ask.

Heat moves into his eyes and I grin, knowing I've got him right where I want him. But then, he suddenly turns the tables on me, taking my power, and before I know it, he's on the bed, and I'm bent over his lap.

"Luke!" I squeal and kick my legs, but my attempt to free myself is futile. Then again, do I really want to break free?

His hand comes down over my ass and I let loose a yelp. "You like to tease me, Katee?"

"Oh my," I say as he rubs his hand over my curvy backside. My sex clenches. No man has ever done anything like this to me before and I think I might…like it.

"Teasing isn't very nice, you know," he says and gives me another smack. It tingles all the way to the needy juncture between my legs. "Girls who tease need to be punished," he says, his voice so deep and hoarse it curls through me and arouses me even more. His hand comes down again. "Are you going to be a good girl from now on?" he asks.

"I'm not sure." I whimper and wiggle my ass. "But I'll try."

"That's not good enough," he says and lifts me from his lap. I stand before him on shaky legs, my panties so wet if he doesn't touch me soon, I might go insane. "Take your pants off," he demands.

"Why?" I ask.

"Because I said so."

My God, I love this sexy take-charge side of him. A little sound catches in my throat as I release the button and pull down my zipper. I wiggle my hips just to tease him a bit as I shimmy my pants to my ankles. I kick them away and stand before him in my damp panties.

He slides a hand between my legs, and feels my wetness. "Take them off," he commands in a soft voice. After I do as he says, he taps his lap. "Lay back down here."

I gulp as I put myself over his lap, and his big hand caresses my ass. "You've been shaking this ass at me all night, Katee, teasing the living fuck out of me."

"That's just how I dance," I say, a half-truth. I love to dance with him, love the way our bodies touch as we move around the floor.

"If I didn't know better, I'd think you wanted me to fuck you here." He spreads my cheeks and runs his finger along my crevice. I quiver as he reaches beneath me, and puts a finger into my wet pussy. I nearly orgasm on the spot.

He fucks me with his finger for a few minutes, then adds another and our moans mingle. I think I'll put my cock in here first, get it nice and wet, then I'll fuck this hot little ass of yours."

"Luke," I say, both excited and terrified by the idea. He rubs the hot bundle of nerves inside me, and just like that, I let go. An orgasm breaks through me, and I come all over his hand.

"Jesus, fuck," he murmurs and grows harder against my stomach as I concentrate on the powerful pulses and marvel at how fast this man can make me climax. He says he's helping me in the bedroom, showing me what I should expect, but when it comes right down to it, I think he's ruining me. I'm pretty damn certain no man will ever live up to his standards.

"On the bed, ass in the air," he says. "And lose the shirt."

With my head somewhere still in the stars, I slide off his lap, remove my shirt and bra and sprawl across the bed on shaky knees.

"Hands over your head," he says.

I reach up and grab the slats, and he shoves a pillow underneath me. He leans into me, puts his mouth near my ear and whispers, "Look at you all hot and ready for my cock."

I gulp for air, my body so turned on, it's hard to breathe.

"Katee, do you still keep your lube in your make up bag?"

"Yes," I whisper. "But how do you know that?"

"I know a lot of things about you?" he says, and dashes into the bathroom. A moment later the sound of him removing his clothes reaches my ears, and by the time he climbs onto the bed, I'm shaking with need. "Your sweet little cunt is dripping," he murmurs as he grips my hips and puts his cock at my opening. He powers forward and enters me in one hard thrust. His curses reach my ears, and I cry out from the pleasure. He rocks into me, the friction igniting my body.

"Oh, God, yes…"

"You like how I fuck you?" he asks.

I swallow against a dry throat. "I love your cock, Luke. I love how you fill me and make me come."

He pulls out and drives into me again. "I want to fuck you everywhere," he says. "I need to." The emotions and urgency in his voice send a little thrill though me. "Tell me you need that, too." He runs his hand along my spine, then puts it between my ass cheeks. He inserts a finger, and I move against him.

"I want that, too," I say. "I want you to be the guy to fuck my ass, Luke. I wouldn't trust any other guy with my body like that." He stills inside me for a moment, and I'm pretty sure he stopped breathing. "Luke?"

"Yeah?"

I move my hips, encouraging him to fuck me. "Harder," I say, and he pulls out and powers back in.

"Put one hand between your legs, and rub your clit for me." I do as he says, and he groans his approval. I move against my hand as he slides his fat cock in and out of me, pistoning hard, and I cry out as another orgasm rips through me. I clench around him, a hot explosion of need.

"That's a girl, get my cock all nice and wet for your sweet ass." He pours lube between my cheeks, and works his finger into my backside, stretching me and preparing me for his girth. After a long time, he pulls from my pussy, pours more cold lube between my cheeks, and presses his crown to my back opening. I go perfectly still.

"Breathe, Katee," he whispers.

I take in a breath as he slowly works his way in. Pain curls around me and he stops moving, giving me time to catch up. He runs his hand along my back, soothing me, and comforting me.

"More," I say, wanting all of him inside me, everywhere.

"You sure?" he asks.

"Never more sure of anything," I say.

He pushes in a bit more and I breathe through the sting as he enters me. "That's a girl," he says, and lightly runs his fingers over my flesh. "I'm in, Katee. I'm all the way in."

"I feel you."

"How does it feel?"

"It feels different. But I like it." I like it so much that a bundle of emotions hits me in the center of my chest. I can't believe Luke is taking me like this. That he's my first. An invisible band tightens around my heart, and tears prick my eyes. Why the hell am I crying? Oh, probably because this man is my best friend, and I want this with him. All of this. Every day. For the rest of my life.

He moves inside me and I lift my hips for him. "You are so beautiful," he says, his voice a low soft murmur that brings on more tears. I sniff, and bury my face in the sheets. The last thing he needs to see is how emotional this is all making me. We're having sex. This isn't about love or the future, right?

His fingers bite into my skin. "You want my cum, Katee?"

"Yes," I say my voice muffled by the bedding. "I want everything," I say, and mean every word of it. I never should have slept with him. It only made me realize how much I love him. How the hell am I ever going to keep my feelings from him? The man can read me like a book. But if I don't hide my emotions, what will become of us? I'll lose my best friend and that can't happen.

He stills inside me and leans over me, his breath hot on my back. "I love that I'm your first, Katee," he says, and his cock pulses inside me as he fills me with his seed.

When he stops spasming, he slowly pulls out, and falls over me. He kisses my back and neck, and I let loose a long sigh. "You okay?" he asks, his voice so achingly tender, my heart misses a beat.

"I'm good," I say. "I think this might be my favorite yet."

He chuckles at that. "I'm going to get you some water and run you a bubble bath."

"Mmm," I say, and stretch out, my body tired from all the physical activity. I let my lids fall shut, and sleep pulls at me, but the next thing I know, Luke is lifting my limp body and taking me to the big Jacuzzi tub. He sets me on my feet and helps me in, then hands me a glass of water. I take a long pull, and he finishes it off.

"Are you going to join me?" I ask. He grins at me, and I

lean forward for him to climb in behind me. He touches my shoulders and pulls me back until I'm relaxed against him. I glance out the skylight and look at the stars. As we lightly touch each other, a phone rings from begins the closet door, and I stiffen.

"That's your phone," I say.

"Leave it."

I crane my neck to see him over my shoulder. His face is tight, the muscle along his jaw clenching. "I think you should at least see who's calling."

"I'm on my honeymoon. I don't have to answer to anyone."

"What if it's Ari? What if she's changed her mind?"

"Let's hope she has," he says under his breath, his words so low, I'm not sure he meant for me to hear them.

As I think about that, my stomach clenches. I want Luke to be happy. And if being with Ari is what he wants, then I have to keep my emotions to myself. But I love him so goddamn much, want him all for myself.

Oh God, Katee, what have you gone and gotten yourself in to?

LUKE

The pool area is set up like a Caribbean resort, with a swim-up bar, and palm trees throughout. There are numerous lounge chairs, and cabana beds around the perimeter, and even tiled lounge chairs set into the pool. I reach for the fruity drink Katee insisted I order and take a sip. It's some concoction with rum and coconut milk. It's not bad, but I could have done without the umbrella.

Tonight we have a nice romantic dinner for the two of us tonight. Afterward, I'm going to have to tell her how I really feel. I'll keep the part about Ari to myself, that it was me who wanted to break up. But by now, Katee has to know what I feel for her is more than friendship, and I'd give my left nut to bet she feels the same way. It's time she knows that what we've really been doing is making love.

She waves to me from the pool as the entertainment director sets up the water volleyball net. I wave back as she swims off with Becca. The two have really hit it off and I wasn't kidding when I said we could visit them in Canada. They swim to the shallow end where a mom is slowly introducing her young baby to the warm water. My heart pinches when Katee drops down to greet the child. The next thing I know she's holding the baby, and the warm smile on her face speaks volumes.

From beside me, Trey stretches out and takes a sip of his beer. I glance his way and before I know it, the conversation has turned to hockey. As it always does. But I don't mind. He's just interested in the game and I could talk hockey for hours.

By the time I turn back to the pool, I see Katee and Becca, along with a bunch of other people, in the middle of a water volley ball game. Katee hits the ball and misses. When she goes under the water, I sit up a little straighter, but then some guy's hands are all over her, pulling her up. She finds her footing, and they both laugh as she brushes her hair from her face. They reset the game and I can't help but notice the douche bag continues to stand close to her.

Anger simmers through my blood, and I work to pull myself together. Like I said, I'm not a violent man, but when push comes to shove, I'll shove. Yeah, I'll shove any guy hovering around my girl, gawking at her like he's looking for a piece of the action.

My girl.

Hell yeah, she's my girl, and it's time she knows it.

That thought gives me pause and takes me back to Ari. What will I do if she ruins my reputation, and gets me fired? Am I willing to take that chance? I worked my fucking ass off to get where I am today, but when it comes right down to it, how is any of it worth it if I don't have Katee in my life and in my bed? I guess I'll have to take a chance and let my skills and reputation speak for themselves.

I sit there for another second, and the game eventually ends. Trey's voice pulls me back.

"What do you say we get in there and mix it up a bit?"

I turn to him and he has a cocky grin on his face. Clearly

he's picked up on my mood, how much I want to punch that guy in the face for touching Katee.

I push from the chair. "Good idea."

A united team, we jump into the pool and go to our girls. The entertainment director makes new teams and the douche bag is now on the other side of the net. Soon enough the ball is in play, and we're all having fun. Katee dunks and I go to her rescue, planting a possessive kiss on her lips when the asshole is looking. Yeah, okay, I'm staking my claim, going all caveman, but I don't give a shit. No man, ever again, is going to touch my girl. If he so much as tries...

"Luke," Katee says, and I continue to hold her against me.

"Yeah."

"The game," she says and Trey nudges me.

"Let's go," he says and sets me up. I spike the ball over the net, but the asshole sends it back, and gains a point.

"Should have stuck me with, Katee," he says and all I see is red.

"I'll set you up again," Trey says, as angry as I am.

The ball goes back and forth a few times, and when Trey sets me up, I jump from the water, and spike the ball over the net—hard—catching the douche bag right in the face. He goes under and one of his buddies helps him. The ref blows the whistle to end the game.

Becca swims up to Trey to congratulate him, but all I get from Katee is one hand on the hip and glaring eyes aimed my way.

"What the hell was that all about?" Katee asks.

I shrug. "Nothing, I just play to win."

She folds her arms. "Luke, are you kidding me? You smacked that guy in the face with the ball."

I look at the douche bag, who's covering his eye as he climbs from the pool. "His face was in the way. I was just playing the game."

"My guy here doesn't even know his own strength," Trey says coming to my rescue.

Katee continues to eye me. "He and his friends invited us all out for drinks tonight."

"Can't," I say.

She narrows her eyes, still assessing me, trying to figure out if I hit that guy on purpose or not. "Why not?"

"We have dinner plans." I drag her to me. "A candlelight dinner is part of the honeymoon package." She frowns, and I cup her chin. She has a strange look on her face, and for once in my life I'm not sure what's going through her head. "What's wrong?"

She plasters on a smile. "Oh, nothing. It's just that the days are going so fast, and soon enough we'll have to get back to the real world. I mean it's not Bali, but still…"

"Maybe that won't be such a bad thing," I say, thinking how we can settle into my place together, make a real home for us. Or if she'd prefer, we can move into a house with a white picket fence, and start filling it with children, sooner rather than later. She might be adamant that she doesn't want marriage, because she doesn't trust guys, but she trusts me, and I saw the way she was with that baby. A niggle of guilt tugs at me and I once again pray she doesn't think of this seduction, or that I didn't tell her the truth about Ari, as a betrayal.

"Back to real life where my phone is ringing off the hook," she says. "I canceled all my appointments at the clinic to come here and I'm going to be working like crazy to catch up."

"You could always come on the road with the team, and work for us." I say, but then I think about her hands on my teammates and suddenly don't like that idea.

"I actually really like my job. I worked hard to get where I am today."

"I know you have."

Her eyes go soft. "I wouldn't be where I am today without you, Luke. You helped me get over all the obstacles." She angles her head and she has a mischievous look in her eyes. "I thanked you for that, right?"

"I can't remember," I say, even though she'd thanked me numerous times growing up. "Why don't we go back to the room and you can show me how thankful you are," I tease. "We have a few hours to kill before dinner."

"A few hours? Really, Luke, that's a lot of time," she says, teasing me. "What will we do for the bulk of it?"

I laugh at her continued teasing. Seriously though, it's hard to last any length of time when it's with her. "I didn't just buy swimming trunks at the gift shop this afternoon," I say, and wag my brows at her.

Her eyes widen with intrigue. "No?"

"No, they had something special behind the counter."

"What are you up to, Luke?"

I pick her up and lift her until she's on the side of the pool, and I jump out beside her. "Why don't you come upstairs with me, and I'll show you."

A fine shiver goes through her, and I grab her towel and wrap it around her beautiful body. I give Trey a nod for helping me, and as he and his wife swim off, I capture Katee's hand, grab our duffle bag full of clothes, and pull her close as we head to the elevator bank. The elevator is waiting as we arrive, and when we get off on our floor, she's shivering. As soon as we enter our room, I flick on the propane fireplace, and place her in front of it until she's warm.

"Let's get a shower, and get this chlorine off our bodies," she suggests. We walk into the bathroom and I turn on the two rain-shower sprays. We strip our wet suits from our bodies, and I lick my lips when I see how pebbled her nipples are.

"Come here," I say and brush my thumbs over her hard nubs before guiding her under the spray.

"So nice," she murmurs as I begin to wash her body. I love how comfortable she is in her skin around me. I mean, I've always seen her in a bra and panties, since it was her favorite outfit around the house, but now she has no trouble being completely bare in so many ways. Once we're rinsed off, I wrap her in a towel and take her to the bed. I dim the lights and her gaze is latched on mine as I walk to the bar, pour us each a drink and take my other purchase from the bag.

She goes up on her elbows. "What do you have there?" she asks, trying to see what I'm hiding behind my back.

I hand her a glass of bourbon, and set mine on the nightstand. "I'll be right back. Drink this, then lay back and get comfortable."

I hurry to the bathroom, take the muscle massaging wand, aka the vibrator, from the package and clean it with soap and water. I rinse it thoroughly, and my heart beats triple-time in my chest when I walk back into the room. The lights are low, most of the glow coming from the fire and the most beautiful woman I know is on the bed waiting for me.

"Hey," I say in a soft voice.

"Hey yourself."

The mattress dips as I sit beside her and run my fingers along her stomach. She shivers beneath my touch. "For a second I thought you were asleep."

"I am sleepy, but I'm anxious to find out what surprise you have in store for me."

I produce the muscle massager wand I secretly purchased and she grins. "You're going to give me a massage?"

I click the button and the end starts vibrating. "They sell these to people who've been skiing all day and need something to relax their muscles. You're always taking care of my body, massaging it when I'm stiff..." She chuckles at that. "I thought it would be nice to take care of you for a change."

Her hand goes to my bare chest. "Believe me, you've been taking care of me."

I smile at that. I like that she feels that way. "Lay back, Katee. Let me relax you."

She rolls over and offers me her back. Her muscles jump at first contact, and then she laughs. "That actually feels kind of good."

"It has a five-star rating," I say. She moans and my dick thickens. "What do you think the five stars mean," I ask as I slowly rub her one shoulder, using a circular motion like the pamphlet instructed. "Do you think it could mean five orgasms?" I tease and her laugh is a little rougher this time.

"I hope so," she says, and I chuckle with her.

"I want you to relax, Katee. Take three big deep breaths and then let them out slowly," I say, using the same tactic she uses with me. She breathes in deeply and lets it out, repeating until her body is like putty beneath me. I look her over and smile. I like having her at my mercy like this.

I run the machine all over her back, taking my time with her until she's a puddle on the bed. I roll it over her ass cheeks, and down her gorgeous legs. Her breathing changes and I think she's fallen asleep a time or two. Good. This is the exact mood I want her in when I make love to her.

When I complete her back, I put my mouth close to her ear and whisper, "Roll over."

"I don't think I can move a muscle," she whispers, and as she shifts, I help her until she's on her back. I look over her body, and reach between her legs to widen them.

He lashes flutter until her eyes are closed and her breathing once again levels off. I slow the power down, and lightly massage her breasts, sliding the tip gently over her nipples until they're hard again. I use the little wand on the fronts of her shoulders, and down her arms. Her soft breathing noises and little moans in her half-sleep, half-awake state, tug at my dick.

Her belly flutters as I lightly roll the tip over her. I change position on the bed until I'm between her spread legs, her soft pink pussy wide open and on display. It takes everything in me not to dive in and taste her, but I want every single muscle in her body tranquil when I take her.

Her thigh muscles clench and relax as I work both legs, and the swelling of her clit, the dampness on her sweet sex doesn't go unnoticed. My goddamn cock is so hard, it takes all my strength to go slow, let her get sleep as I pleasure her like this.

After a long time, when she's relaxed into the mattress, I begin a slow slide up her legs, the soft vibrations of the machine in my hand tickling my balls, and massaging my dick. I circle her clit and her chest rises as falls as she whimpers in sexual bliss. Her dampness grows and I slowly, slide the tip back and forth over her clit. In some dream-like state, she puts her one hand on her stomach, and the other goes to her breast and she strokes her nipple. I want to speak to her, but I don't dare pull her from this trance she's in. I continue to play with her clit, then jack the power a notch. She whimpers some more, and her mouth parts as she licks her lips.

My own throat is so dry I can barely swallow. But soon enough I'll quench myself with her juices. I push one thick finger into her, and her walls close around me as I continue to manipulate her clit. Her hips move, and I glance up to see heavy-lidded eyes straining to focus on me.

"Shh, sleep," I say and her lids fall shut again. I move my finger in and out of her, and while our lovemaking is slow this time, less hurried, it's more profound than anything I've ever felt before. My heart swells in my chest with everything I feel for this girl and my mind goes back to all the years we spent together, everything from the laughter to the heartbreak.

Understanding her body and what it takes to pull an orgasm from her, I apply more pressure to her clit, and work my finger inside her harder. She sucks in a fast breath, and a second later she's coming all over my hand. Her juices are so hot, they singe my skin and zap my balls. I pull the massage wand away and circle her clit, keeping my finger inside her as she comes down from her high.

Her eyes are open again and she has a small smile on her face as she goes up on her elbows. I toss the wand away, give her sex a long, slow lick to quench my thirst, and then slide up her body. My lips find hers and I kiss her with all the love and passion inside me. No way can she mistake the kiss for anything other than love.

Her hands go around me, and run up and down my back. "That was amazing," she whispers. I position my cock at her soaking wet entrance, and slowly slide in. "Yes," she says as she opens for me, welcomes me into her body as her legs wrap around me. I kiss her softly, a gentle slide of our tongues as we breathe into each other. "This is what it should always be like," she murmurs.

"Always," I say, and I hope she means between us.

Her nails lightly claw at my back, her hard nipples scrap over my chest and the sensations rocket through me. Never in my life have I felt so close to her, felt so much need for her.

"Katee," I murmur, as my cock thickens even more.

"Mmm, I feel you. So hard inside my body," she murmurs.

"I love being inside you like this."

"You've been inside me everywhere now," she says.

"Yeah, I like that," I murmur as I pull out and glide back in again.

"Me too." Her head rolls to the side and her mouth opens, but no sound comes when her sex muscles clench around me.

"I love when you come for me, baby."

"It's so good, Luke. I never knew it could be this good."

"I'll always make it good for you, I promise."

"Okay," she says, but I don't even think she heard me because her eyes are rolling back, and her second orgasm turns into her third. My balls tighten, and I want to hang on, give her a couple more orgasms, but that will have to wait until after dinner tonight, because I need to fill her with my cum.

"Yes," she whispers at the first clench. "Fill me with your cum. I love it when it drips out of me."

Christ, her words turn me on even more, and I come harder, spurt all my seed high inside her. Her muscles squeeze me, massage every last drop from my body until I'm spent, exhausted, but my need for her is hardly sated. I bury my face in the crook of her neck, and her hand lightly brushes over my back, stilling as her breathing changes, sleep once again pulling at her.

"Luke?"

"Yeah?"

"I think this might be my favorite."

Mine too, because this wasn't just sex for pleasure, this was lovemaking. I relax over her, my body weight pinning her to the bed. Some small part of my brain reminds me we have dinner reservations. I try to move, but my muscles won't allow me.

"Dinner," I manage to get out, my voice muffled against her skin.

"Order in," she whispers. "I'm not done with you."

Despite my exhausted state, I grin. Because she has no idea just how *not* done I am with her either.

KATEE

The sun is low in the sky, and the cool air whips over my face, but I don't care. I'm having too much fun skating on the outdoor rink to worry about frostbite. I guess I must be acclimating to the temperature here in the mountains.

Luke skates circles around me, and I smile. He's so at home on the ice. He must be anxious to get back to hockey... to Ari. As I think about that, a knot tightens in my stomach. I realize we're just playing here, and soon enough reality will come crashing over me like a bucket of cold water. My mind drifts back to last night and the slow tender way he made love to me.

Made love?

Wait, what am I thinking? That was just another lesson, to show me how good sex was when you were in a sleepy state of mind. Or was it?

Okay, Katee, keep it together. Don't go confusing sex and emotions.

That first night when we watched porn, we talked about that. Talked about how much better sex was when it was with someone you loved. The truth is, I've always loved Luke. I just never let myself *love him* the way I always wanted to, until this week. I consider that a moment longer. Luke has always teased me sexually, but has never made a real pass at me before, or tried to get me into his bed. Is this really about teaching me about sex, or am I just some kind of rebound?

Oh God, am I his rebound?

"Hey what are you thinking about?" Luke says as he comes skating up to me.

I quickly glance around, and that's when I spot the beautiful glassed-in gazebo, a wedding taking place inside it. "Look," I say to Luke. Anything to distract him, before he probes too deep and sees what I'm feeling. He follows my gaze, and takes in the wedding.

"Want a closer look?" he says, and I nod.

We skate to the edge of the rink, and he stands behind me, wraps his arms around my body to keep me warm as the couple inside the gorgeous gazebo exchange vows.

"Why so quiet?" he asks.

"No reason. Just tired out, I guess," I say.

He presses warm lips to my neck. "Have you ever pictured yourself walking down the aisle like that?"

"No, not really. You know how I feel about marriage."

"But you did say you'd do it with the right guy."

I nod. "True." Only problem is Luke is the right guy, he's just not my guy.

We stay there and watch until the rings are placed, and kisses are exchanged. I let loose a sigh, and Luke chuckles against my ear.

"You want that, Katee, and you totally deserve that."

I shrug. "I'd rather elope," I say.

"Liar," he responds, and skates off before I can pinch him. I go after him, my heart a little heavier than it was moments ago. Tomorrow we go home, and in two days, I might lose my only friend. How can I possibly be around him, especially if he gets back with Ari, and pretend there is nothing more between us? I'm not sure I can pull that off.

From the side of the rink I see the guy who I was playing water volleyball with. He waves to me and I wave back. Maybe I should have taken him up on his offer to get a drink. Maybe I should seriously start looking for someone else.

Luke skates back to me, with two cups in his hand. "Hot chocolate," he says.

I take it from him and smell the chocolate. "Mmm," I say, but think twice about drinking it. After a week of indulging, my pants are beginning to tighten.

"Drink it, you're perfect," he says. I shake my head, and wish he couldn't read me so well.

I take a sip from the cup, and warmth goes through me. "You're paying for my extra yoga classes when we get home."

He laughs. "Anything for you, Katee."

"Luke?"

"Yeah."

"Are you worried about going back? Worried about what Ari wants to do?"

He frowns and looks down. Once again, I get the sense that he's holding something back from me. "I'm looking forward to getting back, having some down time," he says.

What about Ari? Doesn't he miss her?

My heart gives a little jolt. Is it possible that after this week, he's come to his senses and sees what kind of girl she really is? I never thought the pampered princess was meant for him. But like I said, I never thought any of the girls he went out with were right for him.

And why is that?

Oh, probably because none of them were me.

I'm in love with my best friend.

Dammit, girl. What have you done?

"I think I'd like to go back to our room. I have some packing to do," I say.

Luke's gaze rakes over my face. "It's our last night. You don't want to do something fun?"

"I'm worn out," I say. "Plus, I want to go into the gift stores and pick up a few things for my mom and some friends."

"Okay, I'll go with you."

I put my hand on his chest, and he angles his head. "No," I say quickly, maybe too quickly, judging by the way his brow is furrowing. Hurrying to explain, I say, "I know you hate shopping, and getting you into the stores to get the swim suit was painful enough. I'll go by myself."

"Really?" he says, and I force a smile, pretending there is nothing wrong with me.

"Yes, really. I might even check with Becca to see if she wants to go with me. She mentioned something about shopping the other day."

That seems to relax him. "Oh, okay. Then I'm out."

We leave the rink, and sit on the bench to take off our rental skates. Luke drops to his knees before me and tears prick my eyes when he begins to loosen my laces. My God, I am so much in love with this man. I take a deep breath and it turns to fog in front of my face when I let it out slowly.

"You are tired, aren't you?" Luke says.

"Yeah," I say, thankful he's mistaken my emotions.

"Let's get room service, then you can hit the shops."

I nod, and he puts his arm around me and leads me back to our suite. The warmth of the place washes over me and I glance around, memorize the place, and all the beautiful things we did in that bed…and that shower.

Luke places our order, and I busy myself with folding all my clothes and arranging them neatly in my suitcase. I flick the TV on, needing the background noise to keep me from dwelling on all the chaotic emotions making me weepy. Soon enough our food comes, and we enjoy a quiet dinner together, the last one we'll have at the resort.

"That was delicious," I say, as I push my plate away.

"Dessert?"

"Hell no." I check the time.

"You're perfect," he says.

I roll my eyes at him. "I'd better get ready to go."

"I'm going to jump in the shower." He bends down, gives me a warm kiss on the mouth, and says, "Hurry back."

He disappears into the bathroom, and when the water turns on, I press my palms to my eyes and work to pull myself together. My mind goes back to all the amazing sex we had this week. As I reminisce, I once again can't help but think last night we made love in that bed.

Is it possible?

The things that man brought out in me, the things he says to me, every time he tells me I'm perfect, I can't help but think he might want more. But I'm so damn afraid to set myself up for failure. What if I say something and he doesn't want more?

What if he does?

My heart leaps at that. Maybe I'm not a rebound, and maybe he was using the lessons as an excuse to be with me. Oh, God, do I dare hope? I stand quickly, and my chair nearly falls backward. I need to talk to him, to find out how he feels. If I don't I could spend the rest of my life regretting it.

I walk toward the bathroom when the suite's phone begins to ring. Who the hell could that be? I change directions head toward the phone. Perhaps it's Becca. Then again, we exchanged cell phone numbers, so I can't see her calling on the landline. I reach for the phone, and put it to my ear.

"Hello."

A pause and then, "Who is this?"

"Ah, it's Katee Williams. I think you might have the wrong room."

Curses come through the line, along with a bit of static. "Where is Luke?"

My heart jumps into my throat. Oh, God, it's Arianna. How the hell did she get this number? Then again, I guess it wouldn't be too hard. A call to the switchboard would easily put her through.

"He's unavailable right now. Can I take a message?" I ask politely.

"What the hell are you doing there with Luke?" she spits out.

"I'm just keeping him company." What the hell am I supposed to say. Oh, I've been having sex with him because you rejected him.

"Of course you are." She laughs. "It's not like I have anything to worry about when it comes to you. He told me all you'd ever be to him was his tomboy friend."

"I...am his friend," I say as old insecurities come rushing back. Did I really think for one minute that he could want more from me? Maybe I really am just a rebound. Someone to lose himself in as he waits for Ariana to come to her senses.

"Tell him I've had enough time to think. I'm ready to walk down the aisle with him."

The room goes fuzzy around me, and I sink down into the chair. I should feel happy. I want to feel happy. This is what Luke has been wanting to hear, right?

"Are you there?" she asks, her tone cruel and impatient.

"I'm here."

"Tell him I called. Better yet, don't. I'll be at the airport waiting for him. I want it to be a surprise."

"Okay," I say, and the other end of the line goes dead.

I sit there for a few minutes, and try to wrap my brain

around what just happened. Ari wants Luke back and is going to surprise him at the airport.

I take a fast breath, then another and another until I feel dizzy. I think back to when we first arrived. I told Luke I was sorry that things weren't the way they were supposed to be. He agreed. Then there was the time I said after one week everything with Ari would be okay, and he said he hoped so. I can't forget the time his cell phone rang, and I said it might be Ari changing her mind. Once again his quiet response to that was he hoped she did. Oh, Jesus, I never should have come here with him. Sure, we might have won the honeymoon couples game, but that's only because we go way back. We're friends, nothing more.

I glance around the room, and the need to flee, to escape the things I'm feeling, pulls at me hard. I jump up, tug on my boots, grab my coat and purse and rush out the door.

My mind is a chaotic mess as I step on the elevator, and the slap of wind when I leave the hotel is a welcome wake-up call. With no idea where I'm going, I walk. Night has fallen over the ski village as I follow the path that leads to the ski hill lounge. I step inside, glance around at all the unfamiliar faces and take a seat at the bar.

The bartender tosses a rag over my shoulder, and glances at me. "What can I get for you?" he asks.

Since I'm going to need something strong to get me thought this, I say, "Bourbon, straight up."

A familiar guy sits beside me and says, "Make that two."

LUKE

Where the hell is Katee?

I glance at the clock. She's been gone for hours now. Ignoring the hundreds of messages on my phone, I try texting her again, but I'm still not getting any response. I call again, but it goes straight to voice mail. Unease morphs to panic, and I pace from the door to the window. It's nearing eleven and I'm pretty sure the shops closed ages ago. Maybe she went for a drink with her new friend, or maybe she's lost or hurt.

Okay, enough of this. I pull on my jeans and a sweater, grab my coat and head out the door. The resort is huge and I have no idea where to look, but decide to head to the shops. I make my way to the center of the village, but the stores are all closed. Jesus Christ. Maybe I should check in with security. As full-blown worry burns through me, I head to the bars. The first few I check, she's nowhere to be found. I start to make my way back to the suite, hoping she's returned, when I hear laughter coming from the ski hill lounge. I turn and follow the path.

I pull open the heavy door, and laughter and music fall

over me. I scan the place, but she's not here. I grip my hair and wrack my brain as I tug. I do another quick scan when a movement catches my attention. Relief washes through me when I find Katee coming from the ladies' room. I lift my hand to wave to her, but she stumbles a bit. What the hell is going on?

I'm weaving my way through the crowd and making my way to her, but stop abruptly when she settles into a chair next to the douche bag from the water volley ball game. Oh, hell no!

As anger burns through my blood, I step up to her. "Katee, it's time to go."

Glassy eyes latch onto mine. "Luke," she says, "What are you doing here?"

"I'm here to bring you back home."

She waves her hand at me. "I don't want to go home. I'm having drinks with my new friend Jacob."

I turn to Jacob who stands to his full height. "Is there a problem?" he asks.

"Yeah, there's a fucking problem," I say. "You're having drinks with my wife, and that's a big fucking problem for me, asshole."

Jacob laughs. "Your wife. The gig is up, dude. She told me everything."

My gaze flies to Katee's, and my heart jumps in my chest. "Katee, what's going on?"

She waves a dismissive hand my way, and turns away. "I told you I'm having drinks with my new friend."

"I think you should come with me."

I touch her arm and she jerks it away. "You can't tell me what to do. You're not really my husband," she says, her words slurred slightly.

"You're not going back to this guy's room," I say blatantly.

"I can do what I want."

Jacob pokes his finger into my chest and sways a little. Looks like he had also had too much to drink. "Yeah, dude, she can do what she wants."

Before I can think better of it, I shove Jacob and he goes flying backward, falling into a table and crashing to the floor. As everyone jumps, the commotion gaining their attention, I use that opportunity to lift Katee from her chair, whether she likes it or not. I hate going all Neanderthal on her, but she's not safe with this guy.

"Luke, don't," she says feebly as I grab her coat and lead her outdoors. She blinks as the cold washes over her and I help her into her coat, zipper it to her neck. "What do you think you're doing?"

"Putting you to bed. You had too much to drink, and I don't want you to regret your decisions come morning."

"We never should have slept together," she says as I put my arm around her waist and lead her along the path. "That's the decision I regret."

I clamp my mouth shut, despite the storm going on inside me, and get her back to our room. Once inside, I undress her, leaving her in her bra and panties, and get her a glass of water. I root through her bag until I find a bottle of acetaminophen and I place it on her nightstand. She falls fast asleep and I slide in beside her. Everything was going so good between us. After her shopping trip, I had planned to tell her all the things I loved about her, tell her what she means to me. But she never came back. I have no idea what happened to her tonight, or why she decided it was a good idea to drink with a stranger in a bar, but come tomorrow morning, I sure as hell plan on finding out.

I close my eyes, and the next thing I know, an agonized moan is pulling me awake. I glance at the clock. Dammit, we slept in. We have a plane to catch in a couple of hours. At least we'll have time to talk on the long flight back to Seattle.

"How are you feeling?" I ask quietly.

"Horrible." She turns to me and her eyes are red, her hair a tangled mess.

"Let's get you in the shower."

She shoves the blankets off, and then winces. "I can shower myself."

As she pushes me away, physically and emotionally, my stomach clenches. "We have to hurry. We have a plane to catch."

"I can be fast."

She walks away from me and closes the bathroom door. Bile punches into my throat at the sound of the lock clicking into place. What the fuck is going on? Why is she distancing herself from me? My mind races as I climb from the bed, and toss my clothes into my suitcase. Is this her way of telling me it's over between us, that we had fun here, but now it's time to get back to the real world? Still, this is so characteristic of the girl I've known since I was a kid.

I finish packing and she comes from the bathroom wrapped in a towel. She continues to avert her gaze as I stare at her, waiting for some sort of explanation as to why she went drinking with a stranger last night.

When she continues to ignore me, I hurry to the bathroom to take a quick shower. I finish and find her sitting at the kitchen table, fully dressed, her head resting in her hands.

"Killer headache?" I ask.

"Something like that," she says and finally looks at me. My heart jumps into my throat when I see the blankness in her stare. Have I lost her as a girlfriend, or worse, as a friend?

"Katee, why—"

"We should get going. We don't want to miss our flight." She stands and grabs her suitcase.

I dress quickly, tug on my winter clothes, and meet her at the door. In the lobby, we call for a car, and I grab us each a coffee and a muffin for the road. She's quiet on the way to the airport, and while one part of me wants to press, to find out what's going on between us, there is another part of me that is terrified of the answer.

We make our way through security and when we're finally in the air, I turn to talk to her, but she has her head resting on a pillow, her eyes closed. From her breathing, I can tell she's still awake. Why the hell is she pretending to be asleep?

Because it's over, dude, and she's trying to let you know that.

Since I tossed and turned all night, sleep pulls at me too. I close my eyes until we land in JFK for our connecting flight. We grab a bite to eat, and every time I try to engage her in conversation, she changes the subject, talking about safe things, like hockey, her work, how busy she'll be when she gets back.

Soon enough, we're on the plane back to Seattle, and once again, she has her head on her pillow. For the life of me I can't understand the change in her. I've always been able to read her but she's put up a wall that I can't seem to climb over.

My heart lodges in my throat. Fuck man, maybe I never should have played a stupid sex game with her. I'm pretty sure I fucked things up between us. I can't let that happen. I can't let anything come between us. She must be pulling away because she only wants to be friends, but can we be friends after this? Have I totally fucked up our lives?

I try to breathe, but my chest is so goddam tight it's hard to fill my lungs. I close my eyes, but can't quiet my mind enough to sleep. My thoughts drift to Ari. As much as I hate it, I'm going to have to face her when I get back. I can only hope she's come to her senses. If not, I'm not sure what I'll do. One thing is for certain, I can't marry her. But will that put my career in jeopardy? I'm so seriously fucked, I don't know what to do.

I'm exhausted by the time the plane lands in Seattle, and

Katee is moving slowly as we make our way to pick up our luggage. We took her car to the airport, and parked it in the lot. From the way she's acting, I'm wondering if she's even going to want to drive back home together. Our luggage finally arrives, and we make our way outside. As soon as I push through the doors, I find Arianna waiting for me.

"Luke," she cries out and throws her arms around me.

"What are you doing here?" I ask, as she peppers my face with kisses.

"I've missed you."

I turn to find Katee, but she's lost in the crowd. I catch a glimpse of her as she heads to the parking lot. "Katee, wait."

She ignores me and panic races through my blood. Arianna touches my cheek. "Forget about her," she says and before I know what's going on, I'm being shoved into a taxi, the driver loading my luggage as Ari slides in beside me.

I try to climb out, but she latches on to me. "What the fuck, Ari."

"I gave you your week, now it's time for us to get back on track."

I let go of the door handle and turn to her. "Is this really what you want? To be married to a guy you don't love? A guy who doesn't love you?"

Her smile drops and venomous eyes glare at me. "We can be good together, Luke."

"No, we can't."

"Are you forgetting that I can destroy you?"

"Go ahead and try. I don't care anymore."

Her head rear back. "You're kidding me?"

"No, I'm not. I'm in love with someone else. I always have been."

Her eyes go wide and she looks out into the crowd. "You can't be talking about that tomboy."

"She's not a tomboy."

"No, she's a conniving whore. That's why she went away with you on our honeymoon. She's been trying to get you in to her bed for as long as I've known you. When I called your room—"

"You called my room?"

The driver climbs in and pulls in to traffic before I can get out. "I wanted to talk to you, to make sure you came to your senses."

"She didn't tell me," I say. Shit, was her change in behavior because Ari had called? "What did you say to her?"

"I just told her that I had a change of heart and wanted you back."

"Fuck, Ari, why would you do that?"

Her face twists into a cruel grin. "Because I'm sick of her. Sick of the way she looks at you."

"What are you talking about?"

"Oh, come on. Don't tell me that you don't how much she loves you. Everyone knows it, Luke. It's rather embarrassing for her. I mean look at her and look at me. There's no comparison."

I shake my head, hardly able to believe what I'm hearing. "You're right, there isn't."

That brings a smile to her face, and she snuggles in closer. "Don't worry about her. I straightened her out and told her that she would never be anything more than your tomboy friend."

Unable to spend one more minute in this car with her, I look at the driver and say, "Pull over."

Ari sits up straight. "Don't you dare, Luke!"

"We're done, Ari." Oh, Jesus Christ, this is such a mess. Katee must think I love Ari, and why wouldn't she? I never should have agreed to Ari's terms; I should have been honest with Katee right from the beginning. But I was too much of a chicken shit, worried that I'd mess things up between us. But

I went right ahead and did that anyway. Fuck man, how the hell am I going to make this right between us?

"I'll ruin you," she shouts at me.

"Fine, but if you do anything to hurt Katee, you'll be sorry."

KATEE

Even though it's the crack of dawn and I'm exhausted, I climb from my bed and walk to the shower. The spray does little to wake me. Then again, nothing has really woken me up from this haze I've been in for the last two days, since I returned from Italy. I haven't heard from Luke, haven't checked any of the social sites. The last thing I want to do is read Kari's blog and find out the wedding is back on.

I turn the shower off, and make my way to the kitchen for some much-needed coffee. I press the button and as it percolates, I pinch my eyes shut, and try to dispel the images of Luke and me together at the resort. I still can't quite figure out how a man in love with another woman could be so passionate, loving and caring in bed with me. That night we made love, well, that was the most beautiful coupling in the world and not something I'm ever going to come back from.

Get it together, Katee, it was just sex.

Then why, oh why, did it feel like so much more? I don't know, but I can't dwell on that. I need to get my life in order and find a way to move on. My coffee maker beeps, and I pour a strong cup and drink it black, needing all the caffeine and none of the fillers. Cup in hand, I walk back to my room to get ready for work. I don't bother with makeup. Heck, who do I have to impress at the clinic anyway? The clients lay on the bed with their eyes closed. It's not like I'm going to find myself a man that way. Not that I want any other man. But then again, maybe I should seriously start looking. It might be the only way I can move on from Luke.

I dress, and don't bother with a lunch, since I'm going out with Michelle, a co-worker. She asked me yesterday, and suggested this new, pretty swank place that opened around the corner from our building. We've gone out a time or two in the past, but we always just grabbed a sandwich, so the switch to a costly restaurant was a bit of a surprise. Nevertheless, I readily accepted. I need the distraction, and maybe I'll find a nice businessman at the new oyster bar. Lord knows, I'm off hockey players.

I grab my raincoat, tug it on, and hurry to my car. I jack the tunes to keep my mind busy as I head into work, and everywhere I look, I think I see Luke. I squeeze my car into a parking spot, and greet Nancy at the front counter as I make my way to the back, to my rented space in the clinic. I ready my room for my first client, and get to work. With a packed day to make up for my absence, my morning goes by quickly. Michelle pops her head into my room as I change the bedding for my after-lunch client.

"All ready?" she asks.

I grab my purse, and my raincoat, and head outside, but it's unusually hot and dry for April. We talk about work as we hurry down the busy sidewalk, and when we reach the new restaurant, I'm quite impressed, although the oyster bar brings back memories of my first night Italy, and my throat tightens. But I don't want to ruin my friend's mood, so I plaster on a smile and grab a seat.

"I think we should order champagne," she says and my head rears back.

"Why? It's only noon on a Tuesday." Then another thought hits, and I lean into her. "Are we celebrating something special?"

"Maybe," she hedges, and I check her finger. She's been dating the same guy for the last few years. Has he finally proposed? But thinking of marriage has my throat tightening once again. I swallow down the knot. I am not about to let my own misery take away from her happiness.

"Spill," I say.

Before she can answer, our server steps up to us. She has a plate with one oyster on it.

"From the gentleman," she says and places it in front of me.

"You've got to be kidding me," I mumble under my breath as Michelle orders a bottle of champagne. A very expensive bottle. She definitely has good news. I glance around the restaurant, trying to figure out who would send me a single oyster. No one is staring back, so I'm a bit confused.

"Are you going to open it?" Michelle asks.

"No, it's probably some creep who trying to get laid and thinks oysters will put me in the mood. What a jerk." I push the plate away, and a worried look comes over Michelle's face. "What?" I ask.

"I think you should open it."

I eye her. What the hell is she up to. Is this part of her surprise? "Okay fine." I grab the shucking knife, and our server comes back with our champagne. I take a sip first, then pry at the oyster with the knife.

"I've never done this before. Oh, wait, it looks like it's already been opened." Michelle sits up a little straighter in her seat, and unease moves through me. What is going on with her? I slide the knife in, twist it, and the shell easily pops open. What I find inside has me completely confused.

"What the hell," I say, and glance around the restaurant a second time, thinking the server made some sort of mistake. The engagement ring inside must be for some other woman. But when I see Luke coming toward me, tears fill my eyes. Is this really happening? I must be dreaming, or at least hallucinating. I briefly close my eyes and open them again, but Luke is still there, closing the distance between us. He comes up to our table, and drops to his knees before me. Everyone in the restaurant turns our way, and a few start snapping pictures, but Luke, private guy that he is, seems oblivious to everyone except me.

"Luke, what's going on?" I ask.

He takes the engagement ring from the oyster shell and holds it out to me. "What's going on, is that I want to marry you, Katee."

"You want me to marry you?" The water in my eyes turns to a steady stream of tears and soaks my face. "I don't understand."

"What's not to understand. I love you. You love me. I want us to get married and have a family together."

I stiffen in my chair, and look around. Am I being punked? "Is this some kind of joke?"

The entire restaurant goes quiet, listening to our very intimate conversation. "It's not a joke, although I've been a fool." He lowers his voice, for my ears only. "Ari never broke off with me. I broke off with her. She wanted to save face, and threatened my career. I promised her I wouldn't say anything. She gave me a week to think it over. I took that week, hoping she'd come to her senses and realize we weren't right for each other. You're the girl I wanted to be on my honeymoon with."

"But...but you said nothing about us being in Italy was right."

"I did," he says and pulls two tickets from his pocket. "Because we should have been in Bali."

I choke on a big fat hiccup. "Luke," I say, trying to wrap my brain around this.

"I haven't been completely honest with you, Katee. You need to know that the lovemaking wasn't really all about me teaching you anything. I was hoping you'd fall in love with me. See how good we could be together."

Lovemaking...

"We are good together, aren't we?" I say quietly.

"I wanted to tell you the truth. I don't like keeping secrets from you, but I was afraid. I was afraid if you didn't feel the same way as I did, that I would ruin our friendship. Losing you would destroy me."

"It would destroy me, too." I put my hand on his cheek. "I'm sorry about our last night in Italy. I never wanted to be with that guy. It's just, after Ari called—"

He presses his finger to my lip. "None of that matters now." He holds the ring up. "This is what matters. Will you marry me, Katee?" he asks, his voice now loud enough for all to hear.

I glance around, take in the spectators. "I can't believe you did this, went through all this trouble."

"I would have done it sooner, but it took some arranging." He smiles at Michelle and that's when I realize she was in on this.

I sniff, and Luke brushes a tear from my cheek. "I'm shocked to be honest," I say.

"You once said romance on screen is better than real life. I wanted to prove otherwise."

My heart fills with all the love I feel for him. "It's quite the grand gesture, and just so you know, everything in real life is better when I'm with you, Luke."

My gaze moves over his face as he looks at me with pure

adoration. I take a moment to think about everything we'd been through this last week. I wasn't a rebound, and sex wasn't just about teaching me what I was missing, it was also about Luke showing me that he loves me as much as I love him.

"Is that a yes?"

"Yes, yes, yes," I say loudly and the crowd cheers as he picks me up from my chair and spins me around.

"Talk about a girl who knows what she wants," he says.

"What can I say, I'm I know a good thing when I see it. That's what you love about me."

When he's done spinning me, he slides the ring on my finger, and says. "You know what I love about you, Katee?"

"What?"

"Everything," he says, as his gaze holds mine. He puts his hand on my cheek. "I love everything about you. I love your smile, kindness, strength, perseverance, honesty, and intelligence. But the thing I love most, is *us* Katee. You and me, meant to be together, forever."

EPILOGUE

Katee

Three months later:

"The ski hill was nice, but this," I say as I look out over the spectacular beach with the pearl white sand, "this is my kind of honeymoon." I turn my head to find Luke grinning at me. We'd only just arrived this morning, and the first thing we did was hit the beach and enjoy the sunshine. A pleasant reprieve after all the rain in Seattle. "Then again, as long as I'm with you, we can make the best out of anyplace."

He reaches out and take my hand in his. "I don't care where I am, Katee. Just as long as you're with me." I frown at that. "Hey, what's wrong?"

"How am I going to handle it when the team goes on the road? I'll miss you."

"Come with me," he says.

I roll my eyes at him. "You know I can't take a baby on the road."

"You're not pregnant yet," he says, although we've certainly been trying. "Come with me until you are."

"I could do that," I say, as my mind going back to Ari's threat of ruining his career. She certainly tried. She'd blasted him on social media, and tried to get her daddy to fire him, but in the end, all she ended up doing was making a fool of herself. Her daddy, tired of her antics, cut her off, and the last I heard she was working retail. I feel sorry for her in a way, and I hope eventually she finds what she's looking for, as long as she stays away from my husband.

Husband.

Will I ever get used to thinking of Luke as my husband? I smile as I think about that, and my mind goes back to our wedding. Luke was right, I did want to walk down the aisle with friends and family watching. My mother was so ecstatic, and Luke's parents, well, they welcomed me with open arms, like they always have. Luke's mother even whispered to me that she hoped we'd finally see how right we were for each other. Luke certainly opened my eyes to that in Italy. Grinning, I glance out at the beckoning water. I stand, and head toward the waves on our own private beachside cottage, giving an extra shake to my backside.

"Keep that up and you're going to get it, Katee Kat."

I shake some more, and when he jumps from his lounge chair, I yelp and run into the water. Luke comes splashing in behind me. I dive under, but he's a strong swimmer and instantly catches up with me. He gathers me in his arms, and presses his lips to mine. I wrap my arms and legs around him, and can feel his erection press against me.

When we surface, we're both gasping for air. "This is perfect, Luke," I say as I glance around, taking in the scenery.

"You're perfect, and I'm going to show you just how much I want you."

He carries me from the water and takes me back to the

cottage, laying me out on our private cabana bed. I shift to the middle, and he crawls between my legs.

"This side of the beach is private, but what if someone comes?" I say.

He gives me a crooked grin, and tugs at my bikini bottom. "Oh, someone is going to come. A couple times."

A little thrill goes though me. "I never had sex outdoors before."

"You're going to do a lot of things with me, baby."

"I'm looking forward to that," I say and release the strings on my bikini top. A growl catches in his throat as I expose my breasts, and I love, absolutely love how much he wants me. We've been having sex like crazy, and yet his hunger for me only seems to grow and intensify.

He stands up, and removes his swimsuit, showcasing his magnificent cock. I can't help but stare at it.

"Like what you see?" he asks.

I crook my finger, to urge him closer. "You know I do."

He falls over me, and his mouth meets mine. I open for him and we kiss with all the love and passion inside us. His mouth leaves mine, and he feathers kisses over my warm body, and I writhe beneath him. My God, the man sure knows how to bring me pleasure.

He kisses my breasts, nibbles on my nipples until pain and pleasure merge. I rake my hands through his hair, and move my hips, showing him exactly where I want his mouth. His chuckle vibrates through me as he goes lower, and that first sweet touch of his tongue to my clit pulls a loud moan out of me.

He feasts on me, his tongue swirling and bringing me insane pleasure. My body heats up even more, and the second he inserts a finger, I come all over him. A cry climbs out of my throat. Honest to God, the man knows how to make me come. I used to tease him about being fast, but now he's the one teasing me.

He stays between my legs, prolonging the pleasure, and when I finally stop spasming, he slides up my body, presses his lips to mine to share the taste. I slide my hands around his body as his gorgeous cock probes my opening. I lift my hips and his groan curls around me as he slips inside. My body opens for him, and we begin moving together, both giving and taking, loving and sharing.

I hold my man to me, and my heart is so full, I'm sure it's going to burst from happiness. I slide my hand between our bodies and stroke my clit, and it does something to Luke. If there is one thing I learned about him, it's how much he loves it when I touch myself. Then again, I love when he touches himself, too. We rock together, and moisture breaks out on his skin as another powerful orgasm rockets through me. His mouth finds mine again.

"I'm there, baby," he says, and throws his head back and fills me with his seed. I squeeze my sex muscle to keep all his cum inside, hoping this time I'll get pregnant. If not, we can keep on trying and I'm okay with that.

He stays inside me until he grows flaccid, then he rolls to the side and takes a big breath. I roll toward him and circle his nipple with the tip of my finger. Goose bumps break out on his skin despite the heat of the day. I give his nipple a little pinch, and he laughs, because he knows he'll get to do the same to me soon enough. I can't wait.

"Luke," I say sleepily.

"Yeah?"

"I think this is my favorite, Luke."

He rolls toward me, and places on hand under his head. "Yeah. You like it outdoors?"

"What I like is making love while trying to make a baby. That's my favorite."

He takes me into his arms and I feel his strong heartbeat as I breathe in his scent. "It's my favorite too, Katee."

I give a contented sigh. "We like that same things. That's what you love about me."

"Oh, you think that's what I love about you?" he teases as he climbs back over me, hard and ready to show me all the things he loves about me.

Thank You!

Thank you so much for reading, **The Stick Handler,** Book 2 in my **Players on Ice Series**. Be sure to check out **The Playmaker**, book 1 if you haven't already, and read on for an excerpt of **The Body Checker**, book 3. I've also included a sneak peek at **Single Dad Next Door**, because I'm totally in love with the story!

Interested in leaving a review? Please do! Reviews help readers connect with books that work for them. I appreciate all reviews, whether positive or negative.

Happy Reading,
Cathryn

THE BODY CHECKER

Jonah:

A loud thump from one of the many upstairs bedrooms pulls me awake. I shift on the sofa, open one eye, and groan. Partly because my place is a disaster after last night's—all night— party, and party because I have a killer fucking headache that's blurring my vision.

I turn over, using slow, easy movements, and the beer bottles lined up on the coffee table sway as I try to blink the room into focus. I steal a glance at the massive clock on my wall, each tick of the second hand amplified in my head as I discover it's just past noon. Christ, I've only been asleep for a few hours.

I close my eyes as I think about finding my way to my comfortable king-size bed, but another loud thump sets off a pounding behind my eyes. I'm going to fucking kill whoever is stomping around upstairs. But when the noise continues, I realize the banging isn't coming from one of the bedrooms, it's coming from my front door.

I drag my hands through my mussed hair, smoothing it

down, and swallow against a dry throat as I try to pull myself together.

Who the hell would be at my door this early on a Saturday morning? All my buddies are asleep in my house. Most have flown back to Boston, my hometown and the spot where I'll be hanging out after a successful season, to celebrate my massive contract extension with the Seattle Shooters, and anyone who knows me, knows I like to sleep in when I'm not on the road.

The knocking continues. "Okay, I'm coming," I yell, and reluctantly climb from the sofa. I grumble under my breath, trip over a pizza box, and stumble to the door. "What?" I asks as I open it, the noon-hour sun burning the shit out of my eyes. I shade my face with my hand, take in the woman on my stoop.

"Jonah," Shari says, and holds a small pink bundle out to me. A small pink bundle that looks as bad-tempered as I feel.

"What's going on?" I ask, as the baby in Shari's arms lets out a loud shriek. Jesus. I falter backward, my head ready to explode from the godawful noise.

"What's going on is I'm tired, Jonah. I haven't slept in four months, and now it's your turn to take care of her."

I squint and look into the baby's blue eyes, take in her tear-streaked cheeks. "What are you talking about?"

"Meet Daisy," she says and shoves the baby into my arms. She cries louder, and I'm sure my head just cracked at the base of my skull.

"Daisy?" I say.

"Yeah, Daisy. Your daughter."

My head rears back. Oh, fuck no. I must be hearing her wrong. Has to be the hangover messing with my ability to comprehend. I pinch my eyes shut and open them again, hoping I'm hallucinating, but nope—Shari and the baby are still there. "What did you just say?"

"Meet Daisy. She's your daughter." Shari pulls a big bag from her shoulders and drops it in front of my bare feet. "You have enough formula and diapers for a couple days. I suggest you do some shopping."

She turns to leave, and I reach out and cup her elbow. "Oh no, no way is this child mine." I try to hand the squirming bundle back, but Shari folds her arms and steps backward, out of my reach.

"Oh, she's yours, all right."

I rack my brain, Think back to the last time Shari was in my bed. "We used protection. I always use protection," I remind her. "You're making a mistake. This kid can't be mine."

"She can and she is." She gives me a look that suggests I'm dense. "The condom broke, remember?"

Wait, was that with Shari?

"No, I don't remember." Okay, I've been with a few girls—or a lot—but I don't remember a condom breaking when I was with Shari. But it's possible it could have. Judging from the bundle in my arms, I'd say it's more than possible. Still, I'm not ready to accept it as truth. I give a hard shake of my head and the room spins around me. "You've got to be mistaken."

"She's four months old, Jonah. A little over a year ago, I was in your hotel room in Philly, and the condom broke."

I remember Philly. Shari had flown there, and we had one hell of a wild weekend, but no way am I ready for a baby, to be a father, which is why I always wear protection.

"Wait, didn't you say you were on the pill?" If I'm remembering correctly, she told me not to bother with the condom, but I used one anyway.

"So you remember that, but you don't remember the condom breaking?"

I search for clarity. Stupid fucking hangover. "I don't

know what I remember. But what I *do* know is, you can't leave her here with me," I say, and hold the baby out to her. "I don't know the first things about babies."

"Then you'd better read a book, or google it." Before I can stop her, Shari races down the front steps and hops into her car. The doors slams and without so much as a glance our way, she drives off.

I stand there, the baby still in my outstretched arms as I glance up and down the street.

What the fuck just happened?

Mrs. Johnson, my next door neighbor, leisurely strolls down her driveway, and when her head angles my way, I step back and shut the door. Shit. Shit. Shit. Now what the hell am I supposed to do?

The baby's lower lip trembles as she stares up at me, no doubt as terrified as I am.

"Hey," I say, because I'm an idiot and have no idea how to talk to a baby. She wails again, and I cradle her in my arms the best I can and pick up the bag. I walk to the sofa, sit down and rifle through it. I find a pacifier, and put it in Daisy's mouth, and for all of one second she's satisfied. But before I can pat myself on the back for a job well done, she spits it out and cries some more.

Fuck me!

Panicked, my gaze lands on my cell phone. I pick it up and do a quick search.

What to do when a four-month-old cries.

Okay, shit, she's hungry, and I have to warm her bottle and test it on my arm to ensure it's room temperature. I find a bottle in the bag and hurry to the kitchen to warm it. Since I'm smart enough to know rubber can't go in the microwave, I unscrew the top and place the bottle inside, nuking it for ten seconds. I bounce Daisy gently, trying to console her as I wait for the microwave to beep.

"What the hell, man?" my best friend Zander says from the doorway.

I turn to him, and I must have panic written all over my face, because his eyes go wide and he hurries across the room, coming to my rescue. Zander has a younger sister, took care of he growing up. Surely to God, he'll know what to do with Daisy.

"Dude, what the fuck?" he asks as he takes the wailing baby from my arms. The microwave beeps and I grab her bottle. I screw the top back on, shake it, and test it on my arm. I have no fucking idea if it's too hot or not.

Zander holds his arm out, and I squeeze a few drops for him to test.

"It's fine," he says, and puts the bottle into Daisy's mouth. Her tears stop instantly, and she gobbles the milk. "You want to explain what's going on here?"

I hold my pounding head and gesture toward the living room, needing to sit before I do a face plant. Zander follows me in. He takes the sofa and I take the chair across from him.

"Shari stopped by," I begin, and Zander nods. He knows who I'm talking about. Shari is a puck bunny, and has slept with almost every guy on our team.

He quirks a brow. "And?"

"And she said the baby is mine." I shake my head, refusing to believe it, or to entertain the idea for one second longer.

"Oh man," he whispers under his breath.

"How did this even happen...?"

"Dude, if you don't know that," he teases.

"She can't be mine, Zander. I always use protection."

"Protection doesn't always work, and sometimes condoms break."

"Yeah, she said mine broke, but I don't remember. Then again, we all got pretty fucked up after kicking Philly's ass."

He nods and goes quiet, the way he always does when he's

puzzling something out. "The condom must have broken, Jonah. I can't imagine Shari would lie about something like that?"

I plant my elbows on my knees and rest my forehead in my hands as my heart beats triple time against my ribs. "Yeah, I guess." Little hungry gulping sounds fill the silence, and the pounding in my head subsides slightly. I look at the baby.

Am I really her father?

"I'm not equipped to take care of a child," I say. Jesus, I was an only child growing up, and pretty much catered to by a doting mom. I'm a little embarrassed to admit that I've never had to care about anyone or anything but myself, and I'd call my mother to help right now but she and Dad are away on holiday for the next couple weeks.

"No, but I know who *is* equipped," Zander says.

I lift my head to find Zander feeding the baby with one hand and digging his phone from his back pocket with the other.

"Who?" I ask.

"Quinn."

The invisible belt squeezing my chest eases, and I nod. As a daycare teacher, Zander's younger sister might be equipped to help, but that doesn't mean she will. She doesn't even like me. Why would she step up to the plate to help out?

I listen to the one-sided conversation, and when Zander ends the call, I hold my breath, praying the news is good.

"She's on her way."

Air rushes from my lungs. "Thank fuck."

"Hey, watch your language in front of the child."

"Shit, right."

Zander glares at me, until footsteps on the stairs catch our attention.

"Zander?" Liz asks hesitantly as her gaze moves around the room, settling on the little pink bundle in his arms.

"She's not mine," he says to the only girl he's ever been serious about. "She's Jonah's."

"You're kidding me." She plunks herself down beside Zander. "I had no idea you had a daughter, Jonah."

"That makes two of us," I say.

Liz gathers her hair and pulls an elastic from her wrist to tie it up. "Who's the mother?" she asks.

I open my mouth but Zander answers for me. "Shari," he says. He takes the bottle from the baby's mouth and puts her over his shoulder. Jesus, he's a natural with her. Then again, his mother left when he was young, leaving her two children behind. Quinn was just an infant herself, and at four years old, Zander had to take on a lot of responsibility. I'm sure feeding his baby sister was one of them.

"Watch and learn, Jonah." He taps the baby's back, Daisy lets out a loud burb. Christ, she could put a locker room full of hockey players to shame. Zander chuckles.

"Does she have a name?" Liz asks.

"Daisy," I say, and Liz makes an aww sound.

She touches the baby's little hand. "That's so pretty." She looks at the baby, then at me. "She kind of looks like you, Jonah."

"She looks like Winston Churchill," Zander says, and Liz slaps him.

"That's awful. She's beautiful."

Zander cradles her in his arms again, and now that she has a full belly, she falls asleep.

I look at the bundle all wrapped up in a pink blanket. No way. Now way can I do this. I try to breathe through a fresh burst of panic. But now suddenly I can't seem to fill my lungs.

"She needs a crib," Zander says.

A crib? Sure, like I have one of those just laying around.

"Can I hold her for a bit?" Liz asks. Zander hands the

baby over, and I root through the bag again, to see what supplies Shari left for me.

"You're not going to find a crib in there," Zander ribs, a crooked grin on his face.

"Funny," I say, in no mood for his humor. I find a few more bottles, a stack of diapers and a couple changes of clothes. What the hell do I do when I run out?

Hopefully Shari will come to her senses by then, and come back and rescue her child. What kind of mother just leaves her baby with a guy who has no clue how to take care of her anyway? Then again do, I even want her to come back after a stunt like that?

Daisy makes a cooing sound as Liz snuggles her, and while I'm terrified of the little bundle, it scares me more to think Shari could have just left her somewhere alone, no one to take care of her. An uneasy shiver moves through me, and as I feel a strange protective tug, Zander points to the bottles.

"You'd better put them in the fridge."

"Yeah." I gather up the bottles and the cans of formula. Needing a moment to myself, to wrap my brain around this turn of events, I hurry to the kitchen and open the fridge. I shake my head when I find nothing but beer and wine. A baby can't live on takeout. Wait, does a four-month-old even eat solid food?

Christ, I am so fucked.

My doorbells rings and I head back to the living room to find Zander opening the door for his sister. Her hair in a frazzled mess, she steps around him, plants her hands on her hips and gives me a scalding glare.

Air leaves my lungs in a rush, like I'd just been body checked. For a tiny might of a girl, her scowl sure packs a punch

She waves her finger at me, her mess of short blonde hair bobbing around her chin. "First things first, if you're going to have a baby in here, you need to get this place cleaned up," she says. I take in the room from her eyes. Empty pizza boxes, Chinese food containers, bags of chips and dozens of bottles are littered throughout the room. Yeah, okay, it's a pigsty, but we were celebrating.

"I'm not even convinced she's mine, Quinn."

The amber flecks in her blue eyes flare bright. Could she hate me any more? "Clean up," she says, "and put a damn shirt on already." She starts stacking bottles in her arm, clinking them together, and Zander reaches for the pizza boxes to help.

I stand there, dumfounded. Wait, Quinn is going at this situation like I'm actually going to keep the child here with me, in my house.

Oh, hell no. I'm not fit to be a father.

"I can't keep Daisy here, Quinn," I say, pointing to the sleeping baby in Liz's arms. "I have no idea how to take care of a baby." I grip my hair. "Jesus, I have a career to think about, and the last thing I want is to be a father or settle down with a family."

She glares at me, and so help me God, if looks could kill, I'd be riding shotgun on the bus to Hell.

"It's too late for that now, isn't it?" she says.

Jesus, does she have to be so mean? Yeah, okay, I know I'm a selfish prick, but at least I know it and don't pretend otherwise. And yeah, she's right. It *is* too late for that.

Quinn:

I'm so pissed off, I'm sure there is steam coming out of my ears. I can't stand for a man to shirk his responsibilities, and seeing Jonah standing there, denying the baby is even his, makes me want to throat punch him.

I've never, for one minute, liked the way my brother or his best friend lived, puck bunnies in their beds every night. At least now Zander has seemed to settle down with Liz. Seriously though, did Jonah not think that it would catch up to him? That something like this would eventually happen? Sure, he's the golden boy of the NHL, but this is reality, and he needs to clean up his act and stand up to be the man Daisy needs him to be. She deserves that much from him. Especially after being abandoned by her mother.

My stomach takes that moment to clench, and I stop what I'm doing long enough to swallow down the pain of my own abandonment. How can a mother just up and leave her child? I glance at the sweet bundle being held by Liz and my heart squeezes.

Jonah must know what I'm thinking because he puts his big hand on my back.

"Quinn, I really appreciate you helping me out like this."

He splays his fingers, and as the heat of his touch goes right through me, goose bumps pebble my skin, despite the warmth inside his mansion.

Honest to God, I hate myself right now. Hate how much I like his touch. He's a selfish prick who cares about no one but himself. How could I ever like a guy like that...fantasize about being in his bed?

I'm such an idiot.

I shake him off me and stiffen. "Let's get one thing straight, Jonah. I'm not here for you, I'm here for Daisy. That poor child can't be left alone with you until you get yourself together and be the father she needs you to be."

He holds his hands up in surrender and steps back. "Okay, thanks for helping, Daisy," he says.

My gaze drops to his bare chest, to the hills and valleys my fingers itch to touch. I briefly pinch my eyes shut and before I can stop myself, I blurt out, "Put on a shirt."

"Okay, okay," he says and darts up his stair. I watch him go, admire his ass in those nice-fitting jeans.

When I look at Liz, she's biting back a smile.

"What?" I ask, and narrow my gaze.

She shakes her head hard. "Nothing."

"That's what I thought."

I carry the empty bottles into the kitchen, and my brother is pulling a garbage bag out from under the sink. "Zander," I say, and he turns to me, a worried look on his face. I drop the bottles into the bag and glance around the kitchen.

"You okay?" he asks

I push crumbs off a chair and drop into it. "Not really."

He sits next to me and puts his hand on my knee. "Sucks for Daisy, huh?"

"Poor little girl." I fight back tears, thinking of my own childhood. At least I had Zander. He was my best friend growing up. It was always us against the world. He took such great care of me, and still tries to. Often, I have to remind him I'm a grown woman now, but I get his sense of duty to me. It couldn't have been easy for him to step into the role of mother at the tender age of four. Dad was never too right in the head after Mom left, working odd jobs to put food on the table. Most times it was just cereal. I guess he did the best he could at the time. Now we're the ones taking care of *him*. Smoking finally caught up to him, and he's battling lung cancer.

"He'll do the right thing, Quinn. He's a good guy. This just caught him off guard. I probably would have reacted the same way."

I blink up at my brother. "Do you think the baby is his?"

"Shari said it was. Why would she lie about something like that?"

"She sleeps around, Zander. It could be anyone's child."

"I know, but she said the condom broke when she was with Jonah, and the timing is right." My brother goes quiet for a second and looks down, like that thought disturbs him. Like he might have had a broken condom a time or two. Is it possible that he has kids out there that he doesn't know about?

"He's going to need a nanny to help out. He can't bring a baby to Seattle when you guys return for training, or take her on the road with him when you travel," I say, understanding hockey is Jonah's life. He might be a selfish prick, but I'd never want to see him kept from playing the game he loves—the only real thing he loves. I personally know how hard both he and my brother worked to get to where they are now. Talent is one thing, but the passion they both have, the drive, the hours they spend training, that's something else altogether, something admirable.

"Yeah. I know," Zander says. "Do you know any good ones?"

"Unfortunately, no. I can put out some feelers at the daycare and help him interview, though. I want to make sure Daisy gets the best."

"Interview for what?"

We both look up to see Jonah standing in the doorway.

"A nanny," I say, and he opens his mouth like he's going to shoot down the idea. Likely because he still can't accept that the baby is his. I glare at him, and his lips pinch tight. "It will take time to find the right person. Weeks maybe."

Jonah rakes his hands through his mussed hair. "Shit." Dark brown eyes lock on mine, and I brace myself because I know what's coming next. "Quinn, do you think you can stay the night to help me?"

"Well, I'm certainly not going to leave Daisy alone. Poor little girl has been traumatized enough."

"Thanks," he says, and Zander squeezes my knee.

I turn back to him. "Go easy on him, Quinn," he says, loud enough for Jonah to hear. "He's terrified."

I angle my head, let my gaze roam over Jonah's face, his tense posture.

Jesus, Zander is right.

Since the two guys met on the playground back in elementary school, they've pretty much been inseparable. I've seen a lot of emotions cross that man's face, and fear was never one of them. It's clear he's desperate for my help.

As a nurturer by nature, something inside me softens.

I stand. "Okay, I'll stay for as long as you need me to. We'll start a search for a nanny tomorrow. In the meantime, we need to get a few things for her. I'll help you, Jonah. I'll teach you the basics."

His brown eyes soften as I walk toward him. I'm about to slide pass him in the doorway, but he captures my hands in his. My gaze flies to his, as his warmth arouses the needy spot between my legs.

"Thank you, Quinn. I promise to make it worth your while."

He's not smiling, and gone is his signature 'Body Checker' toughness. In its place I see genuine appreciation, and it messes with me a little, makes it hard for me to stay mad at the guy who spent a lifetime overlooking me as a woman and always challenged me to contests, like he would one of the guys

"You don't have to make it worth my anything," I say, the fight gone out of me. "You're Zander's best friend, and like a brother to me." Okay, not a brother, not even a cousin. More like my brother's hot best friend who just happens to make my ovaries stand up and do the Macarena. Shit. "It's the least I could do," I say.

"Still, I'll make it worth your while somehow or another."

"Okay, fine." I push my short hair behind my ears and glance around. "Let's get this place cleaned up, then we'll run out together and go shopping. I'll help you pick out everything you'll need." I do a mental list. "Wait, did Daisy's mother at least leave a car seat for her."

He shakes his head.

"Dammit."

"How about this," Zander says. "Write me a list and I'll go get the stuff, while you clean this place up."

Isn't that just like my brother, ready to jump in and help. He's a good guy, one full of integrity and character.

"No, we'll go. She's my responsibility, not yours," Jonah's says, and I'm glad to see him step up. He's no doubt worried about me snipping a few of his beloved body parts. "Maybe if you could just pick up a car seat, then bring it back."

"You sure? I don't mind. I mean, I am Daisy's uncle right? Not by blood, but by brotherhood for sure."

"I think I should be the one picking out her things, bro. But thanks. And make sure you get her the best car seat. I don't care what it costs, safety first."

"Okay, I'll grab the seat and be back shortly."

Both Jonah and I nod, agreeing on something, which is a first for us—and a good sign that we'll get done what we need to get done without too many arguments or challenges.

I head into the living room to find a bunch of Jonah's teammates, along with their puck bunnies, making their way downstairs. I pause and give Jonah a look that says they need to go. Now. He winces like I'd just slammed him into the boards as I take sweet little Daisy from Liz, thanking her for helping out.

Jonah grips the back of his neck with one hand and rubs like he's got a massive knot to work out. His T-shirt stretches over tight muscles as he massages, and it takes everything in me not to gawk.

"So, ah, I guess I have some explaining to do," Jonah begins when everyone stares at the baby, all wide eyed and frightened, no doubt praying she's not one of theirs. "Apparently, I have a daughter," he says, and his gaze flashes to mine for a second, like he's waiting for my reaction. I smile at him for finally accepting the fact that sweet Daisy is his. "Found out this morning."

"Congratulations, man," Luke, a teammate known as the Stick Handler says as he steps up to me to take a peek at the sleeping baby. None of the others get too close, probably because they're worried it will rub off on them or something. I resist the urge to roll my eyes.

"So yeah, no parties for a while."

I clear my throat to gain his attention. His eyes flash to mine.

"Or...ever again?" he asks, obviously wondering if that's what the throat clearing meant, which of course, it did.

"Not as long as Daisy is in the house, and she's your responsibility," I say.

I mull that over for a second. Will having a child to care for change him, shift his priorities? I've seen it happen in guys; not hard-core tough guys who've never had to care about anyone but themselves. Well, then again, that's not entirely true. Jonah cares about his best friend. When my brother was down and out with a concussion, Jonah checked on him every day, and I can't forget that when he was at the hospital, he'd visit the children's ward. Giggles would fill the hall...and my heart.

Jonah's buddies and their girls grumble as they gather up their things and file out the front door. Looking like a kicked puppy—like he's never going to have fun again—Jonah shuts it tightly behind him.

"Back in a few," Zander says, rattling his keys, and he and Liz leave through the side door leading to the garage, where he must have parked his car last night.

Jonah turns to me when we're the only two left in the

house. "Do you want me to take her from you?" he asks, his voice as shaky as his outstretched hands.

"I think we should lay her down," I say quietly. "Let her sleep."

Jonah scratches his chin. "I don't have a crib yet."

"She doesn't move much at this age. I'd put her in a bed, and secure her with pillows, but I'm guessing all the beds have been slept in."

He gives me a sheepish look. "Ah, yeah."

"Then you get the bedding washed and I'll set her up here on the sofa." I walk across the room and set her down. As I do, I note the way Jonah is studying the way I handle her. She stretches out and I tuck her in, place cushions on the outside of her so she can't roll off. "I'd rather have her close anyway. At least until we get a baby monitor and can hear her cries."

"They neighbors can hear her cries, Quinn," he says, and for some reason that makes me laugh.

"You think that's funny?" he says, his mood lightening slightly. "I thought my head was going to split in two." He pinches the bridge of his nose. "How can something so tiny make so much noise."

"If you're looking for sympathy, forget it. Your headache was your own fault, and you can't drink like that as long as you have Daisy."

"I'm never drinking again," he says and holds his head.

I roll my eyes. Haven't we all been there and said that? "Come on, let's clean. You start upstairs, I'll start here."

We both lose ourselves in our duties for the next hour or so, and from upstairs, I can hear the washing machine going. At least we'll all have clean bedding for tonight. I've never slept over at Jonah's place before. I have my own little condo in the city, close to the daycare where I work. Sometimes, though, when my brother is back home in Massachusetts on hiatus from hockey, I'll stay with him in his mansion just outside of Cambridge. He has a massive property, and most times it's empty. He told me I could stay there anytime I want, even open up a daycare in one of the wings. I've been dreaming of having my own business for years now, but it's his place and I don't want to intrude. Someday he'll want to raise his own family in that house.

Me, well...I'm not interested in a family. I satisfy my maternal instincts at the center every day. Zander, though, he's definitely daddy material. Over the years, he's taken such good care of me, has given me so much, which is why I insist on helping him with Dad's medical bills. It's important for me to make my own way in life, and if Zander doesn't like that, too bad for him. He is, after all the one who made me strong and independent. Now he has to deal with that woman, whether he likes it or not.

I finish gathering up all the garbage, wash and dry the dishes, and take a look in Jonah's fridge. I guess groceries are also on our to-do list today. If I'm staying here, I'm not going on a liquid diet.

The only thing I have left to do is sweep the kitchen floor, but I can't find a broom anywhere. I make my way upstairs, to ask Jonah where he keeps it, and find him in his bedroom, sitting cross-legged on his bed with his laptop open. All this time I've been cleaning, and he's been surfing the net?

Anger sweeps through me. "What do you think you're doing?"

He closes his laptop, like a kid caught with his hand in the cookie jar. Since I'm pretty sure that he was watching porn, or something equally dirty, while I cleaned, I step up to him and open his laptop. My heart jumps into my throat when I see his searches.

Babies. Baby food. Baby clothes. How to take care of a baby.

"Jonah," I say quietly, my heart missing a beat.

He slides his legs from the bed and plants his feet on the floor. "I...just didn't want to look like a total moron, Quinn."

I sit down on the bed next to him. "Look, Jonah. I don't expect you to know anything about babies. You were an only child, and were never around infants."

"I know, but sometimes..." He lets his words fall off.

"Sometimes what?" I push.

"Sometimes, when I do stupid things, you're kind of mean and scary."

I laugh, unable to help myself. "Mean and scary? Are you serious? Jonah, you're known as the Body Checker, one of the toughest guys on and off the ice."

He nods, and I shake my head at him. "You're only five foot tall—"

I stop him. "Five foot two, thank you very much."

"Okay, five foot two, but earlier, you scared the team's two hundred and fifty pound defense man simply by clearing your throat. I mean, I love that you're strong and confident—"

I hold my hand up to stop him. "Wait, you love something about me?" I give a very unladylike snort. "That's a surprise. I thought you *hated* everything about me, especially when I beat you at your own challenges."

"Yeah, well, that's true, but I'm just saying you're a strong woman, with a strong personality."

"Thanks to Zander," I say quietly, not wanting to dwell on the past, or how things could have turned out so differently if it weren't for him.

"When you were younger, I used to think your bark was bigger than your bite," Jonah says, nudging me with his shoulder. I rock against him, and become acutely aware that we're sitting on his bed...his nice, comfy bed.

Don't let your thoughts drift, Quinn.

Suddenly I've visualizing me on the bed, a naked Jonah

above me, touching me with those big, calloused hands of his, giving me pleasure unlike anything I've ever felt before.

Shit, I let my thoughts drift.

I clear my throat. "Is that why you called me a Chihuahua?" I ask, trying to keep my voice steady, despite the hot thrum rolling through my body.

His deep brown eyes go wide. "Shit. You knew I called you that?"

I fold my arms and glare at him. "Yeah, I heard it a time or two."

"Hey, it was a compliment." He nudges me again, and I swear to God if he keeps making body contact, I'm going to hand over my panties and beg him to take me.

I give a humorless grunt. "No it wasn't."

"I was wrong though," he says thoughtfully. "I think you can totally handle yourself. You're not a Chihuahua, you're a Ninja Chihuahua."

This time, I burst out laughing. "Seriously, Jonah? Ninja Chihuahua?"

"Hey at least it's better than the names you called *me*. I can't even imagine what you wrote about me in those journals you always had your nose in."

Oh, no, he can't imagine at all.

Thank God.

SINGLE DAD NEXT DOOR

Rachel:

When my bedroom door flies open and crashes hard against the paint-chipped wall, I groan. "Go away," I say, my voice muffled by my pillow. Not that my roommates will listen, even if they can hear me. Heck, I could scream at the top of my lungs and it wouldn't faze them, much less send them running back to their rooms—not when the view outside my window is that *hot*.

Seriously though, sharing a house with four college freshmans is not my idea of a good time, not when I'm a senior and working my ass off to get into law school. But when I left NYU two months before the start of my fourth year and transferred to Penn State at the last minute, this place was all I could find—and afford. Ultimately, Penn State is where I want to do my law degree after undergrad. I just ended up here sooner, rather than later.

Someone tugs at my pillow and I open one eye to see Becca hovering over me. "Come on, Rach, he just took his shirt off," she says. "You're going to want to see this."

Why oh why did my room have to come with the best view of the hot neighbor's driveway?

"Thank God for this heat wave." Sylvie, roommate number two, fans her face with her hand.

I groan and curl up into the fetal position. I just want one more minute in bed without every member of the house in my room. "I. Don't. Care." Well, that might be a lie. I like looking at the eye candy next door as well as they do, but after putting in a late night at Pizza Villa—I seriously have to find a new job—I need all the sleep I can get before class.

"Jesus, would you look at him," Becca says, her voice a breathy whisper as she peers out the window. "Talk about slurpalicious. I could seriously lick that from head to toe, and back up again."

"Leave," I say on a yawn.

Ignoring me, Sylvie squeals. "He's going back into his garage. Damned if he doesn't look as good going as he does coming."

"But I'd rather see him...*coming*," Becca says, and they start giggling.

"Seriously. Are you both twelve?"

"Shh, he's back," Becca says and swats her hand at me, like I'm an annoying fly that needs to be shooed away.

I shift on my bed, not to get a better look outside my window. No, moving has absolutely nothing at all to do with the shirtless mechanic turning my roommates into dim-witted moths. The *only* reason I'm getting up is to herd these girls from my room, and if I happen to get a glimpse of the hot, tattooed, badass daddy next door, well...then so be it.

I rub the blur from my eyes and toss my pillow at them. "Get away from my window, before he thinks it's me." They don't need to know that the hottie's bedroom window is also across from mine, and that late one night, he caught me staring into his room as he walked around in nothing but boxer shorts. Heck, if they knew that, they'd camp out for the rest of the school year, and that was so not happening.

"Ohmigod!" Sylvie leaps back. "I think he just saw me." She puts her hand over her mouth and starts to giggle. Footsteps pound down the hall, announcing the arrival of my other two roommates. I shake my head as they come bursting in.

Kill. Me. Now.

"Is he out there?" Val asks, her big blue eyes wide and hopeful.

"Yeah, but he saw me looking," Sylvie says. Despite that, she edges back around to sneak another look. Megan hurries across the room, and goes up on her toes to peer over Sylvie's shoulder, trying to catch a glimpse without getting caught.

"Do you really think he killed someone?" Megan asks.

"That's the rumor," Val protests, though her tone holds uncertain convictions.

"Then why isn't he in jail?"

"Maybe it was self-defense."

"He's such a badass."

"He's good with his little girl, though."

"Bad Boy Daddy, now that's hot."

"Do you think he'd spank me if I was bad?"

Unable to put up with their incessant chatter and giggles any longer, I point my finger toward the door. "Out. Now."

A chorus of grumbles ensues as they all sullenly walk to my door. Christ, I'm getting that lock fixed, even if I have to eat ramen noodles for the next month.

"God, you're such a grouch in the morning." Becca shoots me a wounded look over her shoulder.

"Doesn't even have to be the morning," Val adds with a hair toss.

"You need to get your nose out of a book once in a while," Megan says.

"What she needs is to get laid," Sylvie informs them all, but her solution to pretty much everything is sex. Problem is, this time Megan is nodding her head in sad agreement as she follows Sylvia out the door.

"I can hear you," I shout after them. I shake my head and my mussed hair falls over my shoulders. "I'm still right here." As I stand there, dressed only in my tank top and underwear, a warm breeze blows in and slides over my skin, a late reminder that I'd opened my window last night before crawling into bed exhausted. Great. Not only could the hot guy working on his car see my roommates drooling over him, he could *hear* them as well. *And* they just announced that I needed to get laid. How freaking mortifying. I stomp across the room and yell down the hall, "And don't bother to close my door on your way out." As usual my sarcasm is ignored.

I give the door a good slam, which helps improve my mood a little. With a deep breath, I turn around, not to see my hot neighbor, but to close my window. No way do I want him hearing anything else that goes on inside this place, or get the wrong idea that I might want him. I don't. Not in a million years.

I'm completely off guys, trying to keep a low profile. After my ex-boyfriend turned violent and abusive, threatening to kill me if I went to the police, I snuck away under the cover of darkness and put several states between us. His was big and hard like my neighbor, his muscles born from rough carpentry work. Last year, when he came to do repairs on the house I was sharing with friends, I was flattered that I was the object of his attention. At first he was doting and attentive, but as time went by, he became possessive and controlling, and I came to find out later, he'd had other charges against him from numerous other women.

Jesus, why am I such a bad judge of character when it comes to men. Oh, probably because my only role model had been a mean-assed, alcoholic father who drove my beautiful, caring mom to an early grave and me out of the house the second I turned eighteen.

If I try hard enough I can still smell the cheap perfume on his shirt when he stumbled in after a weekend-long drinking binge. God, how I hated those women he slept around with almost as much as I hated my Dad. Mom used to try to protect me from his disgusting behavior, but what hurt the most was how dragged Mom down, aging her pretty face far too early.

My heart squeezes as I think about her. She was a good woman, but was too afraid to leave. Running is hard. I get that now. Not that she really had anywhere to run. Our only other relative was my father's mother. She's still alive, living upstate Pennsylvania where my Dad was born. While she liked me well enough, when it came to Mom and Dad, she always took Dad's side. That's how it is with parents, I guess.

I lift my arms, place my hands on the frame, and lean in to give it a tug when the hottie slowly lifts his head. Our eyes meet, hold a moment too long, and I suck in a quick breath as heat zings through me—and dammit, it's not the autumn sun that has warmth pooling between my legs.

OMFG.

With a wrench clasped tightly in his right hand he stares at me, like we're in a goddamn Mexican standoff. I swallow hard, and will myself to move, but can't seem to tear my gaze away. Ah, what was that I said about dim-witted moths?

Close the window, Rachel.

While my brain struggles to call the shots, my body has other ideas. Ideas that involve staying exactly where I am and ogling the hottest guy I'd ever seen. Blue eyes, square jaw, a body I could play Plinko on, and low riding, well-worn jeans that accentuate bulges in all the right places, and holy hell, the man has a lot of right places. Want prowls through me, hitting every erogenous spot along the way.

Just shut the window already.

He shifts his stance and taps the wrench against his leg as he looks up am me. A small grin touches his mouth, and that's when I realize I'm half naked. *Please, ground, open up and swallow me.* After hearing the girls, he probably thinks I'm trying to lure him to my room, fix that dry spell I've been going through. I grip the window ledge tighter and slam it down, putting the brakes on my body's reaction, and shutting out six delicious feet of hard muscle and pure testosterone. This is so not what I need right now. Coffee. Yeah, that's what I need. Lots and lots of coffee.

I hurry to the kitchen and shove a pod into the Keurig. I pour milk into a cup and set it on the spill tray. As I wait for the coffee to percolate, I wander into the main level bathroom and glance in the mirror. I look at myself and try to imagine how I appeared through the blue-eyed mechanic's eyes. I see black smudges under tired eyes, boobs that only look big because I'm slender from work, school and lack of proper nutrition and rest. My hair is...wait... I grab a fistful of my curls and examine them closer. Oh, God, pizza sauce.

Could this day get any worse?

Christ, even if he did hear my roommates, I'm sure he'd never look twice at a girl like me—especially the way I look now. A guy like him probably goes out with women who are a little more put together, sexier. Although I have to say in the two months I've lived here, I've never seen a woman come or go from his place. Still, I'm certain a girl next door who always smells like marinara sauce and pepperoni isn't even on his radar.

Good, because I don't want to be.

The coffee machine beeps and I hurry back to the kitchen. I grab the mug to take a big sip. Heavenly. Desperate for a shower, to wash last night's work from my hair, I hurry back upstairs to my room, hot mug of coffee in hand. I check the time and grab my clothes. Giggles come from Sylvie's room across the hall as I dash into the bathroom. I turn the shower to cool, partly because it's just so hot in the house, and partly because I need to calm my overheated body down. I might be off men, especially big, scary ones like my neighbor, but my body and brain aren't working in sync this morning. Clearly my libido didn't get the memo when I left New York.

I stay under the needle-like spray longer than normal, needing an extra minute to clear my head. When the water turns cooler, I jump out, dry off, and pull on a pair of shorts and T-shirt. I towel try my hair, then tie it back into a ponytail. I forgo makeup. Not only will it melt off my face, I'm not trying to impress anyone or draw any kind of attention to myself. Once done, I grab my purse, shove my textbooks into my backpack, and head for the front door, feeling a little more alive after the coffee.

The hot morning air hits like a slap in the face and I groan. It's October for God's sake. It's supposed to be time for pumpkin spiced lattes. This is more like beach weather. Mother nature needs to get her shit together. I glance at my watch, and judging by the time—thanks to an extra-long shower—I need to get my shit together, too. This morning I'll have to take my car to school, or risk being late for class. The walk to campus is long, around forty-five minutes, but I prefer it on days like today. I need to save my gas money for the colder winter months.

Since my driveway runs parallel to my neighbor's, I keep my head down, toss my backpack into the back seat and climb into the driver's side. Thank God the hottie is out of sight and I don't have to go through the embarrassment of facing him.

I roll my window down and shove the key into the ignition. I turn it, only for the engine to make some god-awful sound and stall out. My heart races quicker. Shit. Shit. Shit. Frustrated, I give the steering wheel a thump with my fist. This can't be happening. I need this car. Need to be able to depend on it if I have to run again. I might be an old junker, but it's all I have. I can't afford a new one. Heck, I'm on such a tight budget, I can't even afford to have this one fixed.

I take a deep breath, throw up a silent prayer, and twist the key again, only for it to cough and gasp, like it's dying a slow and painful death.

No. No. No

A tap comes on the roof, and I turn to see my hot—shirtless—neighbor with his arms braced over the door of my car. He leans down, his beautiful face close to mine. "Need a hand?"

"I...uh...it's not working."

Jeez, way to state the obvious.

He grins, and when I see a cute dimple that contrasts sharply with his chiseled face, I nearly swallow my tongue.

"Yeah, I kind of got that, you know, being a mechanic and all." As he gives off a bad-boy vibe that messes with my common sense, he grabs a cloth from his back pocket, and wipes his hands before leaning into the car, his head practically in my lap.

Holy fuck!

It takes everything, and I mean *everything*, in me not to grab the back of his head and shove it between my legs. My sex practically quivers at the visual. The girls were right. I do need to get laid. I bite the inside of my cheek to stifle the moan rising in my throat.

"What...what are you doing?" I finally manage to ask, and will myself not to writhe restlessly, and show him what a needy girl I really am.

He pulls the hood release, and the front end of my car jumps. His head lifts and once again his face is close to mine. "Popping the hood." He angles his head, and his eyes narrow. "What did you think I was doing?"

Oh, I don't know. Maybe you were taking this opportunity to go down on me.

"Popping the hood," I say quickly, and try not to think of sex. Dirty sex. Take-me-up-against-the-wall kind of sex. Not that I know anything about that. Sadly.

His laugh is rough and deep as he walks around to the front of the car, and I unbuckle quickly. My legs wobble as I climb out of the driver's seat and follow him. He's grinning when I reach him.

"What?" I ask, my voice raspy.

He touches my cracked windshield washer cap, which I happened to repair all by myself. "Duct tape?" he asks, his voice amused.

"Tools of the trade, right," I say and try not to sound as breathless as I feel. A difficult task considering I'm standing next to a half-naked man that I want to run my hands all over. I mean I've seen shirtless guys before, but come on. This guy is like a freaking viking. He leans forward to fiddle with something, and the movement shows off impressive bicep muscles. I break a sweat as his closeness sends shudders of need between my thighs. Honest to God, the man is a work of art, and all I can think of is no-strings sex—something I've never done before. But that's crazy and reckless and so not me. Truthfully, if I knew what was good for me, I'd slam the hood shut and run in the opposite direction.

I'm about to do just that when he says, "Uh, huh."

"Is...is there something wrong?" Is that my voice? Christ, I sound like I'm whacked out on painkillers.

For God's sake, get it together, girl.

He rubs the scruff on his chin, and I step back, needing a

measure of distance before I actually reach out and run my hands over all his hard grooves and deep valleys.

"Plenty," he says again and checks something else. I have no clue what he's doing. I only know that he looks as hot as hell doing it. As he leans over my car, my gaze slides to his ass, committing the way his pants cup his cheeks to memory. The guy could be in a jeans commercial, or better yet, a Calvin Klein underwear ad. I'm a girl, but advertising like that would have me one-clicking the buy button.

My heart hammers as he stands again. He turns toward me, but I'm far too slow to react. His eyes are piercing, almost a deeper shade of blue when my gaze jerks to his, and I can't tell whether he's thrilled or pissed to find me checking him out.

I step closer and look over the engine. "So, what is it?" I ask, disgusted with myself. I should not be fantasizing over this man.

He clears his throat. "I think the first thing we need to do is replace the spark plugs," he answers, his voice a little hoarse.

"Yeah, that's what I was thinking," I say, my head bobbing in agreement.

That grin is back when I look at him. "You know something about cars?"

I shrug. "Sure...and duck tape."

He laughs and says, "It's not..." he shakes his head. "Never mind. So, you agree then, that something's not firing right?"

Firing? Oh, things were firing all right, and lighting up my body like a goddamn Fourth of July celebration.

Damn him.

Damn Mother Nature.

Damn dim-witted moths.

New York Times and *USA today* Bestselling author, Cathryn is a wife, mom, sister, daughter, and friend. She loves dogs, sunny weather, anything chocolate (she never says no to a brownie) pizza and red wine. She has two teenagers who keep her busy with their never ending activities, and a husband who is convinced he can turn her into a mixed martial arts fan. Cathryn can never find balance in her life, is always trying to find time to go to the gym, can never keep up with emails, Facebook or Twitter and tries to write page-turning books that her readers will love.

Connect with Cathryn:
Newsletter
https://app.mailerlite.com/webforms/landing/c1f8n1
Twitter: https://twitter.com/writercatfox
Facebook:
https://www.facebook.com/AuthorCathrynFox?ref=hl
Blog: http://cathrynfox.com/blog/
Goodreads:
https://www.goodreads.com/author/show/91799.Cathryn_Fox

Pinterest http://www.pinterest.com/catkalen/

Hands On

Body Contact

Full Exposure

Dossier

Private Reserve

House Rules

Under Pressure

Big Catch

Brazilian Fantasy

Improper Proposal

Boys of Beachville

Good at Being Bad

Igniting the Bad Boy

Bad Girl Therapy

Stone Cliff Series:

Crashing Down

Wasted Summer

Love Lessons

Wrapped Up

Eternal Pleasure Series

Instinctive

Impulsive

Indulgent

Sun Stroked Series

Seaside Seduction

Deep Desire

Private Pleasure

Captured and Claimed Series:

Yours to Take

Yours to Teach

Yours to Keep

Firefighter Heat Series

Fever

Siren

Flash Fire

Playing For Keeps Series

Slow Ride

Wild Ride

Sweet Ride

Breaking the Rules:

Hold Me Down Hard

Pin Me Up Proper

Tie Me Down Tight

Stand Alone Title:

Hands on with the CEO

Torn Between Two Brothers

Holiday Spirit

Unleashed

Knocking on Demon's Door

Web of Desire